Rue And Roses

by

Angela Langer

Double9 BOOKS

Rue And Roses

by Angela Langer

ISBN: 978-93-71816-60-1

Published by

DOUBLE 9 BOOKS
2/13-B, Ansari Road
Daryaganj, New Delhi – 110002
info@double9books.com
www.double9books.com
Tel. 011-40042856

ABOUT THE AUTHOR

Angela Langer was born on 21 December 1886 in Vienna, Austria, to a family immersed in the cultural richness of the region. Though little is widely recorded about her private life, her work suggests an acute sensitivity to the societal and emotional constraints experienced by women in early 20th-century Europe. She authored the novel Rue and Roses, which reflects a deeply introspective voice and explores issues of family hardship, emotional isolation, and creative longing. The influence of her upbringing in Vienna, a city then steeped in intellectual and artistic movements, is evident in her portrayal of inner life and nuanced class structures. Langer died at the young age of 29 on 25 June 1916 in Kirchberg am Wagram, Austria. Her parents' identities are not widely documented, and her early death likely contributed to the limited recognition her work received during her lifetime. Nevertheless, Rue and Roses remains a poignant record of a young woman's inner world, highlighting Angela Langer's brief yet thoughtful contribution to early 20th-century literature.

CONTENTS

CHAPTER I 7
CHAPTER II 9
CHAPTER III 12
CHAPTER IV 22
CHAPTER V 26
CHAPTER VI 32
CHAPTER VII 39
CHAPTER VIII 44
CHAPTER IX 49
CHAPTER X 55
CHAPTER XI 67
CHAPTER XII 76
CHAPTER XIII 83
CHAPTER XIV 93
CHAPTER XV 101
CHAPTER XVI 106
CHAPTER XVII 111

CHAPTER I

My parents kept a little shop, and adjoining it was our small lodging. The shop contained lots of different things, such as candles, soap, brushes, and many other articles, all of which I regarded with profound respect. Each time that Christmas came round my father used to receive a large wooden chest, of which the opening and unpacking was my greatest joy. Sometimes my father would show no hurry about this to me so sacred a ceremony, and then I used to remind him of it. At last, however, he declared that he was going to open the chest, and after that I got so excited that I hardly knew what to do. I asked whether I might be permitted to help. But my father said that I was a bother and in his way. Fearing that he might dismiss me altogether, I managed to sit still for two minutes; but then I could bear it no longer. I went to fetch a pair of pinchers and a huge hammer, and stood in readiness, long before the chest was opened, with the tools in my hands. Then I watched my father with breathless admiration as he forced a chisel in between the chest and the lid, and very often burst the lid. My heart beat fast for a moment when the white, soft shavings became visible, and the mere sight of the small, brown cardboard-boxes, which my father lifted carefully out of the chest, made me tremble with delight. But the most joyous moment came when I was asked to get a pair of scissors to cut the string which tied the cardboard-boxes. I walked on tip-toe and spoke softly. Then the unpacking of the brown boxes began, and with loving eyes I looked at the figures made out of chocolate or sugar. There were riders with faces so bold that I hardly dared to think of eating them; angels with limbs so dainty and wings so transparent that I thought them to be real; and many other beautiful things. Broken pieces were found sometimes, and my father gave them to me. Although I longed to eat them I did not do so at once, but fetched a twig, or anything that might resemble a Christmas-tree, and fastened the rider, who, with his helmet cut off, looked less fierce now, the colour-bearer who had lost his flag, or the angel with but one arm, upon it. After I had watched them dangling about for a while I took them off again, and there can be but little doubt as to their final fate. My brother joined me in all these things, especially in eating. I remember a Christmas Eve, when I was five years old and my brother four. Father Christmas had presented me with a small wooden doll that pleased me enormously. It had no hair, nor could it move its limbs much, but I hardly noticed that. I sat on the freshly washed floor and played happily. My brother got a knife with but one blade, the kind that is used in our country to cut the grapes with. The next day, when my mother was about to wash us—an operation which was performed on the table—my brother told me that he did not consider my doll to be beautiful, whereupon I answered that I did not think his knife was a real knife. "Shall I," he asked, when my mother had left us to fetch something out of the kitchen, "shall I try it on your leg?" I don't believe I liked the idea; but too proud to go back on what I had stated, I allowed it at once. After that I felt a quick pain, and a few drops of blood showed on the white cloth whereon we sat. When I saw the blood, however, I began to cry, and my mother returned to the room. My brother was frightened too, but he laughed nevertheless, and asked me whether I did believe now that his knife was a real knife. After my mother had bandaged up my leg, she gave my brother a sound whipping with a birch that Father Christmas had left on the previous day for naughty children.

CHAPTER II

One day all our furniture was moved and put on a furniture-van. When everything had gone, my mother took my brother and myself to another house, where we recognized our furniture at once. As it had grown late, my mother gave us our supper and put us to bed. Next morning we were both frightfully busy. We examined the little courtyard, and found a brooklet flowing right through it. Then we discovered a narrow wooden plank leading over to the other side. For a few moments we dared not speak, but looked at each other with grave yet beaming eyes. At last my brother broke the silence, and spoke in a soft, awe-struck voice:

"Shall we?"

"I don't know."

"Why shouldn't we?"

"I am afraid."

"Coward!"

After these last words my brother looked round cautiously and, nobody being in sight, prepared to go over. Seeing his determination I summoned my vanishing courage and held on to his coat, a thing of which he graciously approved. The other side of the yard was certainly much prettier than the one we had just quitted. It is true that it was paved like the other side, but in a corner I discovered some flowers which I thought were the most wonderful flowers that I had ever seen. They grew on stalks, much taller than I was, and were of a colour that reminded me of cinnamon, as I had seen it in my father's shop. But the most wonderful part about them, and that I only found out afterwards, was that they closed themselves up in the evening, and opened again in the morning. That corner with the flowers now began to play a very important part in my life. Whilst my brother was busy over catching flies, or launching a paper boat into eternity, I sat amongst my flowers and never for a moment grew tired of looking at them. They did not, however, belong to us, but were the property of some other people who lived in the same house as we did. And that was the reason why my brother did not pluck them, as he would have done without doubt had they belonged to us.

One day, when we played in the yard as usual, my father appeared all of a sudden and called us to him. It was not often that he left his shop in the daytime, and therefore we felt much surprised to see him. He told us that we had got a little sister. The news electrified us, and we ran into the house. But as soon as we beheld the scrap of a being that my mother handled so carefully, we calmed down considerably and regarded her with critical looks. She was much too small to take part in any of our games, and to bring her over the plank was utterly impossible. So we did not for a long time care much about her, and everything remained as it had always been. My brother and I were together constantly, and I believe indispensable to each other.

When I was six years old my mother sent me to school. I think I liked it very much because of the school-bag, and the things it contained. A book—a single mysterious book—a slate, a slate-pencil. The slate-pencil had a beautiful red paper wrapped round it, and mother told me not to drop it, as it might break. On the day appointed, she took me there herself. My brother also wanted to come, but he was told that he was far too small. He had to stay at home, and I left exceedingly proud. Confronted with the schoolhouse, however, I grew very still. It was a large, beautiful building, with walls so calm and dignified that I was struck with awe. My mother brought me into my classroom, and told me to be a very good girl. Then she left me, and I was alone with the other children. My place was right in front, and next to me sat a little girl with very long, fair plaits, the daughter of one of the teachers. The fact of having so aristocratic a neighbour made me more silent still. I hardly dared to look up; but that embarrassment soon passed away. She herself broke the spell by telling me that she, too, was going to be a schoolmistress some day. Then I told her about our yard, the brooklet, and the plank. She listened very attentively to all I had to tell her, and soon we became great friends. Her name was Hilda. Next to Hilda sat the daughter of a baker, who was called Leopoldine. She also became my friend.

My life had now changed completely. At school we arranged where to meet in the afternoon, and every day grew to be a great event. It happened sometimes that my new friends paid me a visit. Then we played in the yard, and I felt proud of my flowers. But I don't think my little friends really cared for them as much as I did. Both Hilda and Leopoldine were fond of fishing out all sorts of rubbish from the brooklet, and climbing up the wall that separated the houses. Leopoldine came to see me more often than Hilda, who, as I knew and perfectly understood, was not allowed to have many friends. It was for that reason that I hardly ever saw her anywhere but at school. She was the one I loved best. Our meetings, however, were usually held round the church. The church was placed in the centre of a large square, and possessing many a nook and corner, made an ideal spot for all our games. My brother was as a matter of course a very constant member. Another little boy joined us now and again, and then my brother was most happy. He liked boys decidedly better than girls; "girls," he used to say, "are silly."

By-and-by I got to know different people who lived in the village. Leopoldine took me one day to friends of hers, whose little house was situated close to the grave-yard. The man was a dyer by trade, and I thought him very interesting. He had a long beard that was raven black, and hands not a shade lighter. His hands were so black because of his trade. His wife was stout of figure and red and round of face. In one of the rooms there stood a cupboard with glass doors. It contained glasses that were never used, and cups that had flowers and names painted on them. The cupboard soon claimed my whole attention. Whenever we went there again after that first visit, the dyer's wife gave us an apple or perhaps a piece of white bread. She was very kind to both of us, but did not often speak to me. It was chiefly my friend to whom she addressed her remarks. But that I did not mind in the least. I was so happy to sit in front of that cupboard and look at the things. At first I thought everything equally perfect, but by-and-by my attention was concentrated upon one particular piece. This was a small statue of the Holy Mother, dressed all in white except the veil, which was edged light blue. One evening a wonderful thing happened. The dyer's wife talked with Leopoldine, who, by-the-by, fidgeted about on her chair in the fashion that children do, and I stared at the Holy Mother. She seemed to be even more beautiful than ever, and just when I was wonderingly thinking whether or not I, too, might look as pretty with a white frock and the very same veil on, our hostess stepped up to the cupboard, singled out the object of my admiration, and placed herself in front of me. I trembled with delight. Never had I been so close to it. The glass doors had, though kept spotlessly clean, always hidden parts of its dainty beauty from my longing eyes. And now, there stood the woman holding it in her large, red hands, so that the Holy Mother looked whiter than it had done before.

"Do you know anything about the Holy Mother?"

Thinking that she noticed how much I loved the little figure, I grew hot with shame. At last I nodded and said that she was the Mother of Jesus. And then the most wonderful thing happened to me. Pressing the Holy Mother into my hands, the woman said: "There, you may have it." I cannot tell how I got home that day. All I know is that I came home too late, and that my father whipped me with one of those much regretted Christmas birches.

CHAPTER III

Meanwhile another little sister had arrived, and (I believe it was for that reason) our lodging grew too small. The furniture-van stopped once more in front of our door, and two men carried everything away. Our new lodging was most beautiful. At least I thought so. It consisted of four rooms and a large kitchen. My mother took a maid to help her with the housework, and my father employed a young fellow in his shop. The business did well, better than it had done in the beginning, and my parents began to be regarded as "well-to-do" people.

The house we now occupied stood almost next to the house of my friend Hilda, a circumstance deeply appreciated by me. Once when she came to see me, I showed her all over the place, and directed her special attention to a few new pieces of furniture which my mother had bought in order to furnish all the rooms. There was one room that my mother called the "drawing-room," and of which I was extremely proud, although it had nothing in it but a table, a few pictures and a cheap flower-stand.

Whenever I went into this "drawing-room" I felt as if I was entering a church. The same sensation took hold of me when I showed Hilda in, and I was not surprised that she left the room immediately, believing her to be dazzled and overwhelmed.

There was also a courtyard belonging to the house; it was a very large one with chestnut-trees growing in it. The trees were old and had wide-spreading branches. We children loved the place and enjoyed it with all our hearts. In one of the corners there stood a carriage, or rather a manure-cart, which attracted us greatly. One day we pretended to have a wedding. Leopoldine's brother was the bridegroom and I the bride. I twisted a bunch of buttercups into a wreath and took a towel for a veil. After that we took our seats in the cart and pretended to drive to church. With the assistance of the bridegroom I got out again, and the priest (one of the children) performed the ceremony. We had seen many weddings in the village church and did everything in the proper way. When the decisive question was put at last, we both looked very solemn and said gravely, "I will."

On another day I quarrelled with Hilda, I must have said or done something that she did not like, and it was evident that she wanted to make me cross. It happened towards sunset. Hilda stood with her back against the wall of the house opposite to ours and looked at me scornfully. Her mouth was twisted contemptuously, her whole attitude expressed deliberate challenge. For one brief moment we looked at each other like two embittered opponents, but all at once I felt confounded by her words:

"Your drawing-room looks ridiculous."

Never, never before did I feel so utterly unhappy, and I turned away with burning cheeks. My mother was about to call me in, so I hastened towards her. "Mother," I cried, half choked with tears, "Hilda said our drawing-room looks ridiculous." My mother smiled, and as she took me up the stairs into the little parlour, she said: "That does not matter, dear."

Like a child I soon forgot that incident, but afterwards whenever I entered the room in question, I was struck with its emptiness, and tried hard to understand how it was that I had ever found it beautiful; and although my mother had bought a green cover for the table, the reverential feeling that I had experienced so often returned no more.

After a time I no longer liked to go to school, and I do not think that I made any progress with my lessons. My exercises were done only because I was afraid of getting punished. Ambition I had none. Geography and history I did not care for, and doing sums I positively hated. Furthermore, my teacher had found out that I had no voice and consequently excluded me from singing. The only thing that I really liked was to form sentences. But that subject we had only once a week, and it was done in the following manner.—The teacher wrote with his chalk different words on the blackboard, and we had to use them in simple or compound sentences. There was not one word which I could not have brought into a sentence somehow, whereas all the other children sat silent, and never showed any aptitude for the subject. During the rest of the lessons I was inattentive and tried continually to chat with my neighbours. Very often I was punished.

We were also taught scripture every Friday. A young priest whom we called "catechist" came to the school and read the catechism to us. I do not remember whether I behaved any better during that lesson, the only thing I know is that I felt strangely moved when the tall figure of the catechist, clad in a long black gown, entered our schoolroom and took his seat with an air of dignity. In my opinion the young catechist was a handsome man. His eyes were blue, his hair was thick and brown, but his mouth was always shut tightly, and he struck me as hard and proud. When I think of that time, I can see the schoolroom again. None of the children were more than ten years old, and while we sat perfectly still the catechist asked one question after another.

"Who created the world?" Whereupon a young voice answered:

"God created the world."

"What does that mean—to create?" Another voice:

"To create means to produce something out of nothing."

"Must all people die?"

"All people must die."

These last words always occupied my thoughts, and constantly worried me. Sometimes I woke at nights from my slumber, and imagined that I heard the question, "Must all people die?" whereupon a voice answered: "All people must die." After that I felt inexpressibly sad. I sat up in my bed, listened to the gentle breathing of my sisters, and wondered which of us would be the first to die. A maddening fear rushed to my heart when I thought that my father and my mother had also to die some day. I could not go to sleep again, but thought about what might happen if such were the case, and suffered so intensely that I screamed aloud. Then one of my parents came to my bed and tried to comfort me, thinking that I had a nightmare.

The summer always brought to us a most beautiful event. As soon as the long school holidays began, my mother took us to relations of hers, who lived at a distant village. The journey lasted six hours, and we travelled in the post-coach. In reality one could not even call the place a village, because there was only one house, the home of our relations. It was a mill, and all around it stretched the glorious woods of the lower parts of Austria, sometimes interrupted by lovely meadows, where the grass used to grow to such a height that it towered above our heads. Close by the mill flowed a clear, narrow brook, so narrow in some places that we could quite easily jump over it, in others so wide that we had to wade through it whenever we wanted to cross. In front of the house there was a large kitchen-garden that adjoined a still larger orchard, a spot full of ever new delights. At one time an apple-tree, as if to tease us, would let a beautiful apple fall to our feet; at another time the berries of a shrub would at last begin to show their colouring, and then, again, a wild flower that had opened overnight. At the very end of the garden there was also a beehive. Although afraid of the bees we dared to approach them cautiously, and even advanced to the back of the hive, where little glass windows enabled us to observe the dear, diligent creatures quite closely.

Later on, when the children were many and my fathers business slack, these visits had to cease owing to the fact that my parents could no longer afford the price of the post-coach. But the memory of that lovely, quiet spot, connected so closely with a sweet and careless childhood, still arouses sudden sadness and makes me yearn for it.

My mother used to take my brother and myself to church every Sunday, and that place so lofty, so dark, so doleful, and always smelling strongly of incense, made me strangely shy and still. My mother sat upon one of the benches, but my brother and I had to stand with the school children. We were right in front of the altar, and the priest, together with the sacristan, had to pass us when they left the vestry. The priest was the same priest who taught us scripture at school, and I thought him even more handsome in his surplice, made of white lace. As I never managed to remember when we were to kneel during the Mass, I simply imitated the others; but no matter whether I knelt or stood up, I always watched the priest, and followed all his movements. With a feeling of profoundest reverence I looked at him, and saw how he mixed the wine and drank it, how he swung the censer solemnly, how he prayed, with folded hands, out of the holy book, and kissed it reverently at the end....

My brother, as a matter of course, had also started school, and spent most of the time with his schoolfellows. We were not so much together now, but had, nevertheless, plenty of opportunity to quarrel; he grew naughtier from day to day, and my poor mother was unable to manage him. When my father came home in the evening I, in my little bedroom, could hear my mother crying and declaring that she could stand it no longer. Then my father used to grow angry and say that he could not possibly undertake both the education of the children and his business. So everything remained as it had been.

When I was twelve years old a great change happened. My father sold his business, and bought a house (including a business) in a distant little town. Once more all our furniture was removed, but on this occasion it was carried to the station. Strange to say we children were not informed about it until the last hour, so that I had left the church-square the previous evening in the usual manner and never said good-bye to anyone.

It was getting dark when we arrived at Hohenburg; a carriage drove us home from the station, and my father showed us all the rooms of the first floor. Another floor had been added according to my father's orders, but he would not let us go upstairs that evening. My mother put us to bed and told us not to forget our dreams, since dreams dreamt the first night at a place one has never seen before come true. I listened attentively to what my mother said, and on the morrow I pondered over my dream. "Mother," I said, "I dreamt that we had gone back again to Langenau." My mother smiled, shook her head, and said she did not think that my dream could come true.

The first days and weeks passed quickly, and were full of sweet excitement. My brother and my sisters, as well as myself, made new friends immediately, and I do not think that at this time I thought much about my old friends. The people who lived in the house beside us called my mother "landlady," and I believe my mother liked to hear that. She also took a new maid, whom I thought to be a person of great importance. Very often she used to tell me stories about men, and confided in me her approaching marriage. Whenever she mentioned that coming event she looked exceedingly happy and proud, so I came to the conclusion that "to marry must be something beautiful," and wished to marry too. I confessed it to our maid, but she said that I was not old enough.

"How old, then, must a girl be to be able to marry?"

And to this question she replied:

"I cannot say for certain; some girls marry early, some marry late."

I decided to marry early.

After we had been at the new place for a considerable time, I began to notice that something was going wrong. I could see that my father looked thoughtful, even sad, and that my mother cried often. Then my father went away suddenly, and did not return for many weeks. When he came back again, he looked pale and troubled, and my mother never ceased to cry.

One day I went into the little kitchen-garden and wanted to sit down on an old chair which happened to be there. But another girl of my age, who was the daughter of one of our tenants and had hitherto treated me very politely, was already sitting on the chair. She did not get up as I had expected her to do, but crossed her arms above her head and looked at me sleepily.

"Get up!" I demanded sullenly.

"Why should I get up?"

"Because I want to sit down."

"Well, sit down on the ground."

That answer made me terribly angry.

"Get up!" I shouted, and stamped with my foot; "that chair belongs to us!"

The girl laughed, and after a while she said, still laughing:

"Nothing whatever belongs to you; everything has been seized from your people; all you have left is debts."

Then she sprang to her feet, pushed the chair back with such violence that it fell to the ground, and ran off.

I stood like one stunned and could not for a while understand what she had said; but then I remembered how often my mother cried, how sad my father looked, and all at once my veil of ignorance was lifted. I went back into the house, but as shyly and softly as if I were a criminal, and sat down silently on a chair. My mother sat at the table with the youngest child in her arms, and looked at me in surprise. I was generally very noisy, and upset a chair three times before I sat down.

"Have you quarrelled with someone?" she asked.

"No; but I should like to know whether what everyone says is true."

My mother trembled a little.

"What nonsense! What does everyone say?"

"That we have nothing left but debts."

My mother got up from the chair and put the child on the bed; then she pulled the table-cover straight, and stared hard at an empty corner of the room.

"By-the-by," she said, as if she was really thinking of something quite different, "who said that?"

When I had told her she sighed deeply. No other sound was heard in the room.

"Should you like to go back to Langenau?" she asked after a while.

I felt surprised and delighted. Hilda, Leopoldine, the old church, and lots of other things came into my thoughts and made me long for them boundlessly.

"Oh, mother," I cried, "it would make me so happy!"

During the following week all our furniture was moved again and sent away. We were all frightfully excited; only my father was quiet, and looked grave and pale. We arrived at Langenau late in the evening, and drove to a new lodging. The whole village seemed to be asleep, and nobody saw our arrival. We had been away for a year.

I did not like the new lodging; it was underground, and the water dripped down the walls, leaving trails of a dark brown colour behind. I could hear my mother say that the lodging was damp and unhealthy, and that she had never thought one could become so poor. Then my father answered that she must not lose courage, but have a little patience, and he would try to find something better as soon as his business proved to be satisfactory. They spoke for a long time upon this subject, and I understood that the business in question was a new one, and that most probably it would take a little while to get customers.

My chief reason for thinking the lodging horrible was that we were a long way from the house of my friend Hilda. Furthermore there was no pretty courtyard, nor any other place in which we could run about and play. Three other tenants lived in the same house, and my mother told us to keep very quiet, because, if we made too much noise, the people might complain about us to the landlord.

As soon as breakfast was over, I wanted to run to the church-square, partly to see whether everything was the same as it had been before, and partly to speak, if possible, to my friends. Just as I was about to close the door, my mother called me back.

"Where do you want to go?"

"I am going out."

"That won't do," my mother's troubled voice rang; "the whole place looks untidy, and you know that I have no maid. If you want to go out, you must at least take the two little ones with you."

"I will certainly not take them," I said, and tears filled my eyes. "They are far too small for our games."

"I am very sorry, but you will have to play something that the little ones can play also."

At first I would not consent, and decided to stay in; but as it was nearly eleven o'clock, the time when I knew that my friends left the school, I could resist no longer. I took the two little ones, not very gently I believe, and went away. My sister was about two years old and was able to walk, while my brother was still quite small and had to be carried. My sister clung to my skirt, and so we walked along slowly, much too slowly for my impatience. A few people, mostly those who were about to go to their work in the vineyards, looked at me strangely, spoke to each other, and laughed as they passed. I felt as if they were laughing at me, and I was terribly ashamed because I thought they all believed me to be the mother of the two children. It was very foolish of me to think such a thing, but at that time I did not know that a girl of my age could never be suspected of being the mother of children; all I knew was that it was considered a disgrace for an unmarried girl to have a child. My anger concentrated therefore on the two innocent little creatures, and I felt very much inclined to beat them.

We got to the school at last, and I noticed with great satisfaction that the lessons were not finished, and that I was likely to catch my friends. After a few minutes I heard the great noise that was made when the boys were getting ready to go. Then they appeared, pair after pair, and my heart beat faster. After the boys came the girls. First the very small ones, then the class I had been in. Hilda and Leopoldine appeared at the same time, and I trembled with joy and excitement when I saw them coming along in the gay, careless fashion characteristic of children. My time seemed to have arrived. I stepped out of the corner in which I had hidden myself, and called their names aloud. Both of them turned round at once, and dragging my little sister behind me, I ran towards them.

"Anna!" they called, but then they looked at each other and kept silent. I knew at once that something was the matter, and the blood mounted into my cheeks. In order not to let them see my embarrassment I controlled myself, and asked with apparent indifference:

"Where shall we go?"

"We are not allowed to speak to you," said Leopoldine at last; "your father is locked up."

"Was," corrected Hilda softly, and then they ran away before I even knew what they meant. A little boy, whom I had seen in the company of my brother many times before, came along, said something very rude as he passed and put his tongue out at me. But what did that boy matter? What did the whole world matter now? I stood as if I was dazed, and might have stood there longer if my little brother had not begun to cry. That made me conscious of a terrible shame and of a sharp pain in my arm, and I felt that the child was heavy. I noticed also that it was nearly dinnertime and knew that my mother was waiting for me. I called my little sister, who had been ceaselessly picking up stones from the ground, and, avoiding the crowded streets as much as I could, I made for home. My mother was standing in front of our gate, and looking searchingly up and down the street. Having caught sight of us she came to meet me and took the boy from my arms.

"Where have you been?" she asked; "you look hot."

"I am terribly hungry," I said, and slipped into the house while my mother followed slowly with the children. Soon afterwards we sat down to dinner, and my mother was busily preparing the food for the little ones. I helped her a little, handing her a fork, a spoon, or anything that was beyond her reach. After a pause of some length my mother said: "Did you see any of your friends?"

"No," I replied without hesitation, hastily swallowing a large mouthful. I could feel how the blood rushed back into my cheeks, not because I had told a lie (I often told lies), but because I heard the cruel words hum in my head again.

"You are getting quite a big girl now," my mother continued after a pause, "and you could make yourself very useful at home, if it were not that you have to go to school again."

A silly, incomprehensible fear immediately gripped me. Until that moment I had not thought of having to go to school again. "Mother," I said, and lifted up my arms imploringly, "pray do not send me to school again."

"You are getting more and more lazy; you ought to be ashamed of yourself."

"So I am," I answered rudely.

My mother got up from the chair suddenly, and I thought that she was going to beat me for such an impudent answer. But she did not beat me; she bent down to one of the little ones and, with her face turned away, told me to clear the things from the table.

During our stay at Hohenburg I had scarcely learnt anything, and when my mother took me to school the next day, the headmaster found that out at once. He declared that I was not by any means able to join the fourth class, but must take up the third class once more. My mother never understood why I looked so exceedingly happy when the headmaster told me that.... I was now at least spared the company of those "two." The mere thought of them became unbearable to me. I decided never to go near them again, and to avoid everything that could bring me into touch with them. But if it happened now and then that we met during the recreation, which we had all to spend out in the garden, I quickly looked in another direction. Hilda and Leopoldine were together almost constantly, and it was only sometimes that I met Hilda by herself. She passed me then with eyes cast down, but inwardly I felt that she loved me still and only did not speak because she was forbidden to do so. At such moments I loved her more than I had ever done before; I even thought of walking up to her and speaking to her again. But whenever I wanted to put that thought into action, my feet refused to move; I stood like one rooted to the ground, and all that I was able to do was to look after her and watch how she went away slowly, sometimes very slowly.

One day I heard from a schoolfellow that Hilda had been sent to Krems in order to join a seminary for school-teachers. After that I felt as lonely and wretched as a child has ever felt. It is true that she had never spoken to me again, but her figure was the most vivid picture in my mind, and to watch her secretly from behind a quiet corner had filled my heart with a happiness strangely sweet and sad.... "Why," I thought angrily—"why was Hilda sent away? why not Leopoldine?" Whenever we met, her face wore a malicious smile, the very smile it had worn when she had said those terrible words to me. I began to hate her, and prayed every night to God that He might cause her mother (she had no father) to be locked up too. But her mother never got locked up. One day when I accidentally passed their house I saw a lot of labourers busying themselves over it, and when I, driven by curiosity, stole by in the dusk another evening, the house looked more beautiful than ever. Henceforth Leopoldine was dressed in very pretty clothes, and the smile on her face grew more and more malicious.

I had no pretty clothes, and my parents had no pretty house. My father's business went from bad to worse, and he himself grew to be taciturn and did not speak to us children for weeks. Another little brother had arrived too, and my mother worked incessantly. I assisted her by minding the children and carrying about the baby, but I did not like doing it and felt utterly unhappy.

My brother had been sent to the High School at Krems because my mother had set her heart upon it. My father used to point out to her that he was hardly able to afford the expense, but my mother responded that Charlie was the cleverest boy that could be found, and that it would be an everlasting pity to bring him up otherwise. After these explanations my father was silent, but I am perfectly convinced that he would have much preferred to apprentice my brother to some trade. Charlie came home every Sunday and left again on the Monday. On these visits he treated us all in a most conceited manner, and even declared one day that country-folk were fools. In spite of that I used to see him off each time he went away, and felt like crying when the train had steamed out of the little station.

CHAPTER IV

Without being able to give a satisfactory explanation of my feelings I grew unhappier from day to day, and at times when I was most sad I became conscious of a story in my head, and wrote it down, but tore the paper up again without ever showing it to anybody. My dearest wish was to be sent to Krems, so that I also might join the seminary for school-teachers, and I wondered in my heart of hearts whether Hilda would speak to me then. As a matter of course that secret longing was in vain.

The time when I was to leave school approached at last, and I hailed that event with great delight, for I rejoiced at the thought that in the future I should not be compelled to meet Leopoldine. I had time to spare now, but I did not help my mother with her housework any more than before. I did not like staying at home, and wanted to go away. But whenever I mentioned the subject my mother declared that she could not spare me yet, and that in any case I was too young to face the world alone. I felt exceedingly impatient, grew very discontented, silent towards my mother and my two bigger sisters, and spent, in spite of the noisy company around me, a very lonely life. My poems were the only joy I had; they used to come again and again, but I kept them as secret as before.

During the course of these events I had entered on my fifteenth year, and into my discontent and restlessness there began to twine themselves the thoughts, the dreams, and the wishes of a girl of my age. I knew that all the girls who had left school with me were already associating with young men, and I wondered which of the young men of the village I could love. But I soon discovered that there were none at all who pleased me, because they were all very rude, and constantly alluding to things which made me blush. Contempt and disgust were the only feelings they aroused within me, and it was clear to me that Langenau did not hold the hero of my dreams.

The young men themselves hated me. Whenever they spoke to me I responded shortly and tartly, and if any of them tried to pinch my arm or stroke my cheek, I stepped back and uttered an angry exclamation. After that they used to say that I had better not be so affected, if they were good enough to look at me despite the fact that my people were deeply in debt. I was perfectly used to such words, and knew that those who spoke them were speaking the truth, since the same thing was said at home without anyone contradicting it.

Owing to the fact that my father could afford the fees no longer, my brother had been compelled to leave the High School, and was serving his time in a business.

I suffered under these conditions more than I can ever say. My only wish was to go away from Langenau and to live in some place where nobody knew me and where nobody could reproach me. But my mother would not hear of such a thing. Whenever I spoke about it she comforted me with the idea of getting away later, and I gave in, simply because I could do nothing else.

It was one of my daily occupations to chop up wood in a little shed. The shed was situated at the back of the house, and close to the wine-cellar that belonged to the landlord. Wealthy people from Vienna or the surroundings used to buy wine from our landlord, and not infrequently a gentleman went down into the cellar, and with the landlord sampled the different wines. One afternoon I was chopping wood again—I loved doing it merely because I was all alone in the shed, and my thoughts could come and go undisturbed. I stood with my back against the door, and was both chopping and thinking diligently when a shadow fell suddenly across the wooden sides of the shed; and turning round I saw one of the gentlemen who used to visit the wine-cellar. He smiled at me and started a conversation—whether the rough work pleased me, and so forth. First I felt ashamed of having been observed, but his winning, open manner soon banished my shyness. While he was speaking he smiled and entered the shed. But in spite of his friendliness I felt all at once terribly afraid. I lifted the chopper as if to protect myself, and said: "Will you please go out?" He smiled with even more friendliness, and I saw that his teeth were white and even.

"How shy you are, little one! all I should like to have is a kiss."

I pressed myself hard against the wooden wall, set my lips tightly, and raised the chopper higher still. He must have read in my face something of my determination, because he started to whistle suddenly, and went out of the shed, going backwards as he left. I would have killed him had he dared to touch me.

A young man visited our village sometimes in order to collect sums of money due to a life insurance company. My parents were in no way insured, but every month the people next door received a call from him. One day, instead of the young fellow, a smartly-dressed man appeared who told our neighbours that he was the manager of the company, and that he himself was collecting on this occasion, because frauds had been discovered in connection with the young fellow who had collected previously. After he had left them he knocked at our door, and entered in the politest fashion possible. He looked so very smart that my mother wiped a chair with her apron and invited him to sit down. It was summer, and very hot. The manager seemed to be tired, and asked for a glass of water. After my mother had filled one of her best glasses with clear and cool well-water, he emptied it at one draught, after which he stretched his legs and glanced searchingly through our little room, that looked poor indeed but was kept very clean. My mother, who is but a plain woman, felt much flattered at the sight of his unmistakable comfort, and tried in her humble way to draw him into conversation.

"Dear madam," the manager said at last, "do you by any chance know of a young girl who could help my wife with her housework?"

I sat at the window with a half-knitted stocking in my hands, and slowly let it sink.

"What I need," continued the grand gentleman, "is a nice girl who will mind the children and make herself generally useful."

My mother was just going to say that at present she knew of nobody, but that she could make inquiries if the gentleman wished—or something of that sort—when I got up and, standing before the manager, said: "Perhaps I could be of some use to you?"

Scarcely had I uttered these words when I felt terrified at the courage I had shown, and thought that I must have said something very silly and rude. The manager, however, did not seem to have the same idea, because he smiled and nodded his head.

"That would be excellent," and, after a little pause, addressing himself to my mother, he asked, "When could she come?"

I was quite prepared to hear my mother reply that I could not go at all, or even to see her bursting into tears, and was therefore greatly surprised at what she replied: "If you really care to try her, I could send her next week."

At these words I scarcely managed to suppress a cry of delight. The gentleman then said that he lived at Krems, and that I could come home sometimes. The day of my arrival as well as a few other things having been settled, the manager bowed himself out. As soon as the door had closed behind him I glanced rather shyly at my mother, but she looked into my eyes steadily and said: "As you absolutely will not stay at home, it is best that you should go soon to see for yourself what the world is like." And after a moment she added: "Perhaps you will have good luck."

During the rest of the day I tried to do everything I could to please my mother. I sang the youngest child to sleep, and told the elder ones stories. In the evening when the children had gone to bed, I promised my mother that I would work hard and try to save up a little money. When my father came home and heard of my decision, all he said was that he hoped I could stand the hardship of service.

The week passed rapidly; my mother washed and ironed the few pieces of underclothing I possessed, and I mended them as much as possible. I would have liked very much to buy a little trunk, but my father said that he had not enough money, so I packed my belongings into brown paper, and tied up the small parcel with a thick string.

The manager had arranged to come and fetch me himself. On the appointed day I stood in my Sunday dress and a faded straw hat, which I had decorated with a new bright ribbon, awaiting him in our best room. He arrived very soon; my mother had laid the table, and brought in the steaming hot coffee and some appetizing white bread. After the manager had helped himself to enormous portions, he prepared to depart. I had neither touched the coffee nor the bread, feeling sick at heart, although nothing could have induced me to make such a confession. Several times I ran into the kitchen as if to fetch something, but in reality I wanted to wipe away the tears quickly and secretly. The parting came at last, a scene that could only be a simple one to such a simple woman as my mother, although behind her coloured frock the dear, faithful heart trembled and ached....

"Be good," she called after me, and I nodded back this time with tears in my eyes.

CHAPTER V

The people to whom I went were Jews. The mistress with her dark hair and dark eyes seemed beautiful to me. The four children—three boys and one girl—had all rather reddish hair and freckles, except one of the boys, who was seven years old and idiotic. I had to take the three elder children to school and fetch them home again, to tidy the rooms and to keep the kitchen in order. The lady did the cooking herself. As the idiotic boy did not go to school, he was constantly around me and chattered to me all day long in unintelligible sentences. Often he tore off his clothes and ran about naked. In the beginning I was afraid of him, but I soon noticed that with the exception of a few disagreeable things, to which one had to get used, he was perfectly harmless. Many times during the day he would come and spit into my face. At first I could hardly bear this, but by-and-by I got to know his movements, and quickly turned away when I saw him coming. But worse still than this poor boy was his brother, a boy of twelve years, who had a horrible way of speaking to me, and made me feel as much as possible that I had to obey him. The girl I liked the best.

I had not been in this family for two months when I noticed that the circumstances of the manager were no better than those of my parents. People frequently came to the door and asked me if they could see the manager. But as soon as I announced such a visitor the manager became furious, and told me to tell the people to go to hell. I soon got to know that these were all creditors asking for their money. It had been decided that I should receive eight shillings each month, and I could scarcely wait the day on which my wages fell due. When I left home I only possessed one pair of shoes, and these were almost in shreds. Therefore I thought of getting a new pair of strong shoes and also a small notebook into which I could copy my verses, which, although my work was plentiful, I did not stop writing. But yet I felt as lonely as before. I could easily have made acquaintances, but I did not wish to. The cook at the next house often spoke to me, and told me once that every second Sunday she went out with her sweetheart, who was a corporal; after which she asked me how many times I went out. I told her that I did not go out at all, and at this she looked at me with suspicion.

"Well, I never! then madam very likely allows your sweetheart into her drawing-room to visit you, eh?"

"You impudent person, I have no sweetheart!"

At these words she gave a jeering laugh.

"So it is as far as that already. You are sick of men; I expect one of them has left you in the lurch."

Without answering I turned my back on her, and afterwards we saw each other as little as possible.

I began to hate everybody with whom I came in contact: the baker because he had always some nasty words ready, which made me cast down my eyes and caused the blood to rush to my head; the milkman for the same reason; and the family itself because it was plain that the man was a liar. To my great disappointment I had not received my wages, and so I wrote my verses, which were even more frequent now, on paper bags that had previously contained such things as rice, tea or sugar; and these verses I carefully kept and put away.

One day I had just come back from a walk with the children, and after I had put the youngest child into the cot I went into the kitchen to warm his milk; on entering the kitchen whom should I see but Madam standing calmly in front of the drawer in which I kept my belongings. The drawer was open and my mistress held in her hands one of those paper bags that I knew so well. I was frightened and furious at the same time, but the respect which, at least outwardly, I had for that very indiscreet person prevented me from uttering any angry exclamation. With an amused and astonished face she turned towards me and held up the bag, "You have never told me about these things," she said, seeming not at all troubled at being detected in that mean action. "If you please," I answered, trying to get hold of the bag, "it would not have been worth the while." She still wore the amused smile on her face. "No, let me have it, I am going to show it to my husband."

"For God's sake, no!" I cried in dismay.

"Why not? I like the verses very well."

The whole of my indignation and feelings of revolt immediately vanished. I felt like kneeling down and kissing the hem of her dress; her words had made me very happy, and from that day forward I recognized in her my guardian angel.

The fact that I as yet had not received my wages made me, it is true, feel very sad; but I told myself that this must be the manager's fault, for he ought to have provided her with the money to pay her servant. But she, and of this I was perfectly sure, never even caught sight of a single penny.

My mistress had shown the manager some of the verses discovered in the drawer, but he had laughed and responded that she had better not turn my head altogether since I was a good, hard-working girl, and that there were a far greater number of good poets than good servants in existence. The manager had to go away to Vienna nearly every week. One day when he had gone there as usual and the children were put to bed, Madam came down into the kitchen where I was busily washing up, and said: "Anna, I want to speak to you."

I thought that she was going to pay me my wages at last, and my heart beat faster. She sat down on a kitchen chair, and watched me silently for a while. Suddenly she began again:

"Tell me why you have not been truthful with me?"

I was startled and looked at her in surprise, but my conscience was clear, and so I answered quietly:

"I don't know what you mean, Madam."

She tapped the floor impatiently with her feet, and said:

"No pretences, please. You remember that you told me once that you had no sweetheart, but that poem"—and oh, horror and dismay! she held up a paper bag on which I had written only the day before, and which I had never intended to show to anybody—"that poem does not say the same. Where is he? What profession is he in? Have you got his photo?"

I took my hands out of the hot dish-water, and covered my face.

"Don't be so silly," she continued. "I am a married woman, and you may trust me. Now, come, out with it," and while she said that she looked at me half commandingly, half lovingly. My hands dropped, and I noticed how very red and ugly they were. A new shame overcame me.

"It is true," I said at last.

"That you have got a sweetheart?"

"No; I mean that I have not got one."

"But this poem?" and, greatly puzzled, she looked down at the bag that was smelling of coffee.

"I don't know who he is, nor where he is;" and with sudden courage: "all I know is that he does exist."

"But, pray, where have you seen him, then?"

"I have never seen him at all, except in my thoughts."

"Oh" she exclaimed, and rising with a yawn, she began to leave the kitchen; but at the doorway she turned round once more and said: "As long as you know him only in your thoughts he can do you no harm."

Scarcely had the door closed behind her, when I flew at the drawer, pulled out the bags, and threw them into the fire. I watched until the flickering flames had destroyed every bit of them, then I leaned against the grey wall of the kitchen and wept bitterly.

Oh, for those tears in that grey kitchen! Oh, for those dreams in that grey kitchen! Every moment my heart yearned in incomprehensible longing for him. When would he come? Oh, when? When would he come to take me away, like the princes came in the fairy tales to woo a shepherdess or a kitchen-maid? I felt so sure that we were destined to meet some day, but it seemed a long, long way off. Sometimes a doubting fear would overcome me. How if the picture of my dreams—that picture so proud, so far away—should never turn into a form of flesh and blood, but ever be a dream! At such moments I was weak and foolish. I looked down at my hands, which were so red and ugly from washing-up and scrubbing. If no man would ever love me because of my red and ugly hands, what then? At that question my soul trembled, and tears thronged into my eyes. The next second, however, I smiled at my fears; a line or two out of my poems had fallen into my thoughts. What did it matter that my hands were red and ugly? What did hands matter at all? What had the heart, the mind, the soul of a man or woman in common with his or her hands? The man of my dreams was not a man who would love a girl only for her beauty. No; he would love me for the purity of my thoughts, the chastity of my longing, and for that wonderful part of my being that made me write my poems and dream all day.

Once on washing-day I was standing at the tub, when the door opened and my mother came in.

"Mother!" I cried, "why did you not write that you were coming?"

"We have not heard from you for so long, and when no letter arrived yesterday I became worried, and walked over," she said.

Only then I noticed her tired face and the dust that covered her rough shoes.

"Do you mean to say you walked all that distance?"

"Yes, I did;" and after a little pause; "we must be very careful with our pennies, business is so bad now."

I tried hard to keep back my tears.

"If I only had some money I would gladly give it to you," I said.

My mother shook her head.

"Don't be silly. You need your money yourself. Have you managed to save a little?"

"No," I answered very slowly.

"Let me see, you have been here for a year now"—she began to count by the aid of her fingers—"and your wages are eight shillings a month." She counted again. "That ought to have left you something. I am afraid you are careless, my dear."

Seeing that she looked at me with tender but reproachful eyes I cuddled down beside her.

"No," I said, "I am not careless; but—"

And then I told her that I had never received my real wages; only just enough to buy some very necessary articles of clothing, or to have a pair of shoes mended when it was urgently required. I felt very much ashamed to tell her this, since my own stubbornness was the cause of it all. My mother sat still, and after a long while she said:

"I am glad I have come. I have never been quite at my ease, and wanted to see for myself whether you are happy or not. I have heard of a very good situation, which would be suitable for you. You would have to look after three children, and to help the cook with the scrubbing. The household there is kept on a big scale, and you would learn a great deal."

I remembered the mad boy, who still managed to spit at me occasionally, and the sneers of the older boy.

"I would like to take that place," I said at last.

My mother got up from the linen-basket on which she had been sitting.

"It is easy enough," she replied. "I have arranged for a fortnight's notice with the manager, and if I give it to-day, you are free to go in two weeks' time. I have seen the lady of the other post; she is very kind, and does not mind waiting another three weeks. You might just as well come home for a week. Does that suit you?"

I nodded in silence, and we parted.

When I went into the kitchen later on, my mistress was sitting near the fire as if she had been waiting for me.

"I am sorry your mother wants you to leave me, but I have always said that this was too rough work for you. I hope you will like your new situation."

After the fortnight had passed I again packed up my things into brown paper, but the parcel seemed to be smaller than it had been a year ago. When I took my leave my mistress handed me ten shillings, and promised to send on the rest of the money due to me. Although I knew for a certainty that she would never do it, I thanked her very much for the ten shillings, which seemed to be an enormous sum.

CHAPTER VI

I noticed slight changes when I arrived home. The lodging was the same, but I missed several pieces of furniture, which I knew had formerly been there. At first I wanted to ask for them, but a strange sensation of fear and cowardice closed my lips. There was also a pipe lying on one of the shelves.

"Who smokes a pipe?" I remarked.

My mother threw a quick glance at it.

"Father, of course; he thinks a pipe comes cheaper."

There were also other things that I thought surprising, but I would ask no more.

"I dare say you know that Charlie has left his master," said my mother.

"How should I know? Nobody has told me; where is he?"

"With father; I expect they will come in soon."

Although I felt pleased to see my brother again, of whom I had heard nothing all the time he had been away, I was not pleased that he had broken off his apprenticeship and had to begin afresh.

My mother had started to put the children to bed and to lay the table. When it was dark my father came in with my brother, and after the simple greetings were exchanged we sat down to supper. I noticed now how handsome my brother had become. Although he was only sixteen years of age, he was much taller than my father, and of such gracefulness that I could hardly take my eyes from him. His face was very beautiful. His eyes blue and large, and shadowed by most exquisite lashes. On his upper lip a fair, downy moustache showed, but his under-lip was, I thought, just a little too full.

"What are you going to do now?" I asked him once during the meal. "Speaking frankly, you are too big (and too handsome I had almost added) to be an apprentice."

"You are right, my beloved sister," he answered with a touch of scorn in his voice; "for that sort of position I have grown too big and, to tell the truth, too superior."

"Too superior?" I asked in amazement, and noticed how white and beautiful his hands were. He looked at his well-kept nails thoughtfully for awhile.

"Yes, too big and too superior to have my ears boxed."

"Did they?" I gasped, not daring to complete my sentence.

"Yes, and that's why I ran away."

"Perhaps you ought to have stayed there, after all," remarked my mother somewhat timidly. "What will you do now?"

He gave my mother a look that alarmed me. It was an ugly, almost threatening look, which robbed his face of all its beauty. But as if conscious of the impression produced upon me, he calmly leant back on the wooden chair and smiled self-contentedly.

"There is no need for you to lament," he said, addressing my mother; "I shall not be a burden to you.... I am going to Vienna," he finished, turning to me.

"To Vienna?" I asked. "What are you going to do there?"

He smiled again, and on this occasion contemptuously.

"I don't know yet; but there is no need to worry about such a fellow as I am; it is true that I have no money, but here (he pointed at his forehead) I have got something that is worth more than money," and after this introduction he started to picture his future.

"To begin with," he said, "it is undoubtedly a great misfortune to be born in the country. Think of the vast possibilities that are open to you in town. There are the well-managed schools, the places of historic importance, the innumerable means of earning a living, and the very air of culture and refinement that envelopes everybody. There is no real work in the country, and there never will be. It is true that the people get up in the mornings and try to do what there is to be done; but where is, I ask you, that race of all the different brain and bodily powers that is so characteristic of life in town, where the clever man is superseded by the cleverest man, and everybody tries to reach the top in consequence?... If I were silly enough to stay at a little country-place, what would become of me? Nothing but a mere loafer, who drags about quite uselessly the great gift of intelligence that fortune (my dear, I am above that nonsense of God and Church) has bestowed upon his cradle or rather upon his brain. I have therefore decided to throw in my lot with the quickest and cleverest of my age, and it must be hell itself playing against me if I do not succeed in getting enough money to enable me to buy a few hundreds of such dens"—he looked round the room contemptuously—"in a couple of years."

With my hands folded almost devoutly I sat silent during the whole of this speech, and did not quite know what to make of it. I greatly admired the graceful flow of his words, as well as his thoughts which were entirely new to me. Nevertheless there was something within me that warned me not to surrender the views and ideas I had so far held.

"I hope you will have good luck," I said at last when he made a little pause; "but I should like to know what you are going to be."

"Alas!" he replied, "I can see for myself now that you are not much better than these folks"—he pointed with his thumb at my parents—"and that you have never, not even in the least, raised yourself above the level of your birth. Your way of thinking is the way these folks think"—he pointed at my parents again—"and they think as their grandparents did. Progress is to all of you as foreign as China. How can you be so silly," he continued, somewhat more gently, "to ask me what I am going to be? How can I tell to-day? At the present I have not the faintest notion of the conditions and circumstances of Vienna, and how am I to know which of my capacities is likely to be the most eminent? Let me have the choice of a profession, the possibility of a trial, and I will tell you what I am made of."

Greatly ashamed of my ignorance, I was silent again.

"If you possessed brain," my brother continued—"a thing which I am sorry to say I do not suspect you of after I have had the pleasure of exchanging these few words"—he bowed ironically—"you might have perceived by now that I am no ordinary person, but of an artistic turn of mind. These people"—he pointed again at my parents—"have, unfortunately, little or no understanding of that, and will in all probability fail to comprehend the greatness that the future holds in store for me. That is, however, of little consequence; it is you whom I expect to escape from your present station in life"—I admired the delicate way in which he referred to my station—"as soon as possible. It is true that you will never succeed in reaching the height destined for me, but you may, nevertheless, go on to perfect yourself in every way possible, in order to spare me the distress of blushing for your ignorance and social standing later on."

My father had got up from the table some time before, and with his hands crossed on his back nervously paced the room. He coughed now and again, as if something irritated his throat, and it was plain that he was angry. All at once he stopped in front of my brother.

"Don't you think," he asked, "that it would be best for you to mix with your own class of people as soon as possible?"

"Why, of course," my brother replied with utter coolness, "I have already decided to leave for Vienna to-morrow; all that I must ask you is to let me have the money for the journey, a sum so trivial that I can repay it to you multiplied a hundred times in a few months."

They looked quite calmly at each other, but it was a calm that seemed to be loaded with thunder and lightning. My mother must have felt the same, for she got up rather hastily, and her voice trembled as she said: "There is plenty of time to settle that to-morrow. You had better go to bed now."

The thunderstorm, however, broke next day. My brother insisted on a certain sum of money, which my father thought too great and refused to let him have the whole of it.

"Do you want me to reach Vienna without a single penny in my pockets?"

"I will give you as much as I can spare; there are the little ones to be thought of; I cannot let them starve."

"Then you wish rather that I should starve?"

"I don't think that it would come to that. You are old enough to earn your living."

"Old enough! Do you really mean to say that a fellow sixteen years of age is old enough to earn his living?"

"Why not? I myself had to leave home when I was only a child of eleven, and have worked for my living ever since."

"Worked for your living!" my brother cried scornfully. "Wasting money and getting into debt to such an extent that no dog will take the trouble to look at us. Do you call that working for your living?"

The veins showed thickly on my father's forehead.

"You wretch!" he cried, and flew at my brother's throat, "is that what I get for having taken endless trouble to bring you up?"

It was evident that my brother had not expected so violent an outburst on the part of my habitually gentle father. He grew deadly pale and tried to free himself from my father's clutch.

After he had succeeded in doing so, he reached for his hat and turned to the door. But, before he closed it behind him, he said: "You will find me in the Kamp, if you should happen to look for me to-morrow."

What he called the Kamp was a river of considerable depth. After he had left, the room looked a picture of misery and grief. My mother was leaning against the wall weeping violently; my father was pacing the room, his face rigidly set and breathing rapidly; the smallest of the children, roused by the noise, had started to cry; and I trembled in every limb with excitement.

It was my brother's last words that worried me beyond expression—"You will find me in the Kamp, if you should happen to look for me to-morrow."

I imagined him plunging into the dark green water, sinking slowly and being found entangled in the tall reeds near the banks. "Mother," I said, speaking incoherently and almost inaudibly, "do you think that he will?"

"Don't ask me anything," she replied; "I am the most unfortunate woman under the sun."

During the whole day I hoped that he might still come back. He did not return, however, and when evening drew near I dismissed all hope of ever seeing him again. The next day I could not remain indoors any longer, so I went out and walked towards the river without actually knowing or wishing it. Every time I saw a group of people coming towards me I stopped in terror, for I believed that they had found him. Nobody, however, seemed to be on so terrible a mission.

The people looked gaily at me, and passed on to their work in the vineyards. When I reached the church square, the very sight of which was enough to arouse such sad and sweet memories that I felt more wretched, my brother appeared on the scene. Giving a joyous exclamation, I hastened towards him.

"Where did you spend the night, Charlie?"

But this question did not seem to please him.

"I certainly expected more tact on your part," he replied, stepping over to my side, "than even to allude to that distressing scene at which you were unfortunate enough to be present."

I did not dare to ask another question, and walked along in silence. Secretly I was surprised at his composure.

"I am extremely sorry for your misfortune," my brother said after a pause. According to my opinion it was he who was the more unfortunate of the two.

"Why are you sorry for me?" I asked him, and regretted the question the next moment, because his face flushed with anger.

"How can you ask why, when you yourself were present at this miserable occurrence, which must have taught you of what low descent you are."

"I?"

"Well, of course I mean we, but as I have ceased to belong to these folks any longer, I cannot help feeling extremely sorry at the thought that you will have to spend the whole of your life amongst these narrow-minded people, who are little better than savages. Ever since yesterday I have thought how I could help you."

According to my opinion he needed help far more than I did; but he did not seem to think so.

"What I have decided to do is this: I will take you down to Vienna, where I shall watch over you, cultivate any abilities that you may show—in short, educate you. As soon as I have shaken my boots free from the dust of this place and reached Vienna, I am going to work day and night in order to save enough money to enable me to write for you, and to let you learn all the important branches of art and science, such as languages, music, etc. Do you agree to it?"

I felt mightily touched at his generosity and could not speak for a while.

"As a matter of course," he continued hurriedly, "that cannot be done right away; you will have to wait a little, and in the meantime there is nothing to prevent you from accepting the place that mother has found for you. Your leisure time, however, I want you to fill up usefully, so that I shall not be ashamed of you when I introduce you to my friends. I strongly advise you to read Schiller. There is everything in his dramas that you may need to appear clever and witty in whatever situation you find yourself. It would be an excellent thing if you could quote from his works at every possible opportunity. I also advise you to read Goethe's works. Be careful, however, not to quote from them, as your mind is not yet ready to fathom the profound depth of his thoughts, and you might fall into the evil habit of quoting passages at quite inappropriate moments. Perhaps it is better for you to refrain altogether from reading his deeper works, until I myself shall be able to expound them to you. But," and a very winning smile parted his lips, "it is now time for me to say good-bye."

"Good-bye!" I exclaimed; "where do you want to go to?"

"I am travelling down to Vienna."

"But you have got no money!"

His lips closed, and the winning smile vanished.

"I can see," he retorted, "that you are backward in every way. The thing you most lack, and that you need to acquire first, is tactfulness. Because, alas! one of our family happens to have no feeling at all, do you really expect everybody to be in the same miserable state? Always be careful, I tell you, about mentioning anything that might recall occurrences or situations of a distressing character. A certain pride exists, which is alive even within the most pitiable wretch ... take care never to rouse that," and holding out his hand, he said good-bye.

I did not take his hand, but stared at his beautiful fingers.

"I don't mean to hurt your feelings," I said almost crying, "but how can you get to Vienna without a single penny?"

He frowned, and his handsome face darkened.

"It seems that I cannot expect from you that delicacy of feeling which you must possess if you are ever to deserve my affection. But since you are my sister, and really not to blame for your imperfections—because it is the duty of parents to attend to their children's education, and yours, I mean ours, have neglected that important thing entirely—I will answer your question about the money. You are perfectly right in suspecting that I have not a single penny, but let me tell you that I would much rather walk all the distance from here to Vienna than bring myself to accept another sou from the man who, on account of a strange accident, is entitled to call himself my father. I have tried to find out when the goods-train leaves for Vienna, and have decided to hide myself in it."

I shook my head in horror.

"No, never!" I cried; "you must not do that. I have got some money," and I pressed the rest of my ten shillings, which I had carefully wrapped up in a piece of white paper, into his hand; whereupon I detected signs of both anger and pity on his face.

"Surely," he said, "I should be a scoundrel of the meanest order if I touched this small sum of yours. Far be it from me to do such a thing;" and he put the money back into my hand. "It is true," he added, "that you have shown great tactlessness again, but I will forgive you this time."

Almost immediately he was gone, and although I was standing in the street, I began to cry most piteously, regretting my poverty, my lack of nobleness, even my very existence. I felt convinced that my brother was not only an artist, but also a hero and a martyr.

CHAPTER VII

The situation in which I started soon after these events differed somewhat from my first one. There were only three children, a second maid—the cook—and instead of eight shillings I was promised ten shillings a month. My duties were the same as before. I had to wash up the dishes, to scrub the floor, and to take out the children as soon as I had finished the housework. My new charges behaved much better than the children of the manager, and I liked them all very much. The cook, too, was nice. Neither in speech nor in manner was she objectionable, and sometimes I used to read out my poems to her. She seemed to be very fond of the verses, and often asked to hear them again. That made me very happy.

But after some months had passed away, and I became used to the change, I was conscious again of the old well-known feeling of dissatisfaction and loneliness. Frequently I used to sit down in a corner and sob without knowing what was the matter. I was careful not to let the mistress see my tears, but could not always hide them from the cook, who was nearly always with me. She had asked me already what I was crying for, but I could give no explanation.

One Saturday afternoon, when we were busily scrubbing the floor and all the different meat-boards in the kitchen, the cook noticed my swollen eyelids again.

"What is the matter with you, I should like to know," she said. "You are home-sick perhaps."

I shook my head slowly and thoughtfully.

"I don't think I am home-sick, but I believe I am unhappy because I can't go and learn anything."

"Can't go and learn anything!" she repeated. "What on earth do you want to learn?"

I hesitated a little.

"I am sure I don't know. All I know is that I am frightfully silly."

"Well, I shouldn't say that," she replied good-naturedly. "I quite like the way you help me in the kitchen."

"Oh well, yes; but I mean that I don't know how to play the piano, nor how to speak French."

"But you do not need such things in service."

"Quite so; but I don't want to be in service."

"Oh!" she exclaimed, and then there was a long silence.

After we had done our work we took off our wet overalls, and put on clean pinafores. The cook reached down one of the shining saucepans hanging on the walls, and began to make the coffee, while I went into the dining-room to lay the table. After I had taken in the tray with the hot milk, the steaming coffee, and the cups of white porcelain, the cook and I sat down in the kitchen to take our coffee also. The cook poured out the coffee, and I noticed that her hands trembled a little. She did not speak, and I was silent too, but I could feel that our previous conversation occupied her thoughts. When her cup was empty she put her head into her hands, and looked me straight in the face.

"Then you want to know French?" she asked abruptly.

"Well, it need not be exactly French."

"What else, then?"

"I don't know."

"That's silly. You must know your own mind, to be sure."

"I believe that I should like to learn English," I confessed, much embarrassed and ashamed.

"I have never heard of a person learning English. Why would you not rather learn French?"

"No," I said slowly but decisively, "I would much rather learn English."

"I have thought of everything," she continued after a pause; "the mistress must not know about it. She herself has never learnt anything of that sort, and would consider it to be nothing but pride on your part. But it might be managed, nevertheless, if you would learn only in the evening after you have put the children to bed."

"Of course," I cried delightedly; "I would not dream of doing it during the daytime. There is only one thing," I added thoughtfully: "where shall I be able to find a teacher in the evening?"

"A teacher!" cook exclaimed in utter surprise; "do you mean to say that you want a teacher?"

I lost heart considerably at her question.

"Of course, I am sure it is impossible without a teacher."

"But won't that be too expensive?"

I assumed great indifference at her remark.

"I don't think that it could cost much," I said.

"How much do you think he would charge you?"

"I don't know exactly, but it won't be above a shilling or two."

"But, my dear, you can't afford that."

"Well, let me see. My wages are ten shillings a month, and I do not need all the money."

"Of course not But you have to think of the future."

"Well, that's just what I am doing."

The cook did not understand what I meant by these words, and as the bell rang to show that I was wanted, we dropped the subject, and I did not dare to touch upon it again in spite of the growing impatience and longing within me.

A few days later, however, it happened that the cook spoke of it again quite abruptly.

"Do you think that you would get some benefit from it?"

"From what?" I asked, and looked as if I had no notion of her thoughts.

"From the English language, of course."

"Well, if I knew how to speak it correctly I am certain that I could make a lot of money with it."

"Where?"

"Not here, of course," I replied, and turned my head guiltily away from her gaze. We had to do the scrubbing again, and the cook devoted herself to the work almost savagely; but when the kitchen glittered and shone, and we were once more sitting down to drink our coffee, she continued:

"You must try to take your lessons on a Friday evening. The mistress as well as the master are at the club, and won't be back before eleven. Do you think you could be back before then?"

I was happy beyond expression, and would have liked to put my arms round the neck of that dear simple creature.

"What do you think!" I exclaimed, wild with joy, and with my hands folded as if in prayer; "I shall be in much earlier than that." But in a moment I grew worried again. "Are you sure that the porter won't tell about it?"

"Never mind about the porter. I will have a talk with him."

After that we decided that I should look out for a teacher, and the matter was settled. On the following days when I took out the children, I looked up and down the houses most carefully, and found at last what I was searching for. "Languages and Music taught here," stood out clearly from a black board of granite, and the black board was fastened on to a stately house. In spite of the shyness caused by the grandeur of the house I longed to go in right away, but the presence of the children kept me from carrying out my wish. They were old enough to understand everything, and there was not the slightest doubt that they would go and repeat my conversation with a teacher of "languages and music" to their mother. It is true that my mistress was always most kind to me, but, as cook remarked, she would never have understood.

When I arrived home I told my friend about my success, and asked her how I could manage to go there without letting anybody know.

"The only thing you can do," she said, "is to peep in when you go to fetch the milk."

I thought how very ridiculous it would look for me to go into a room with a large milk-can in my hands, and did not like her proposal. There was, however, no other way if I did not want to arouse suspicion, so next day I pulled the bell of the imposing house. I could hear it ring from within, and the sound made me still more uncomfortable. I wished the milk-can at the bottom of the sea, and while I stood there waiting I thought for a moment of hiding that disgraceful thing. I looked round for a suitable corner, but then I was afraid that it might be stolen, so I kept it in my hand, and only tried to hide it as much as possible behind me when the door opened and a maid asked what I wanted. Colouring deeply, I told her why I had come, and she begged me to step in. She led the way into a room, which I thought was the most magnificent room I had ever seen. There was a very large looking-glass, and the very first thing I saw in it was myself. The second thing I saw was the milk-can, and I looked away quickly; never before had it seemed to me so big and ugly. A few minutes passed, and still I was left alone. Just when I was beginning to regret that I had come at all, the door opened, and a slender, sweet-looking woman entered the room. The lady was Risa de Vall, the teacher of music and languages. As soon as she saw me she smiled a very faint little smile, which I thought was due to the milk-can, and in my heart of hearts I reproached that article bitterly.

"I am told that you wish to take lessons in the English language; is that so?"

"If you would be so very kind."

"Do you live with your parents?"

I blushed with shame, but answered truthfully:

"No; I am in service."

She was silent for awhile, and looked at me with keen, searching eyes.

"Very well then, my hours are from eight o'clock in the morning till six o'clock in the evening. When do you want to have your lesson?"

"Oh, I am so very sorry, but I cannot come before eight in the evening."

And, after I had said that, tears filled my eyes.

She smiled again, but that time so kindly that I felt certain the milk-can had no part in it, and to my greatest delight I heard her say:

"I suppose I must make an exception for once, and give you your lesson at a time convenient to you."

With some hesitation I asked for her terms, secretly fearing that it might not be possible after all.

But I was soon relieved. After looking at me once more very keenly, she named a price that even I considered ridiculously small.

When I repeated this conversation to the cook, she looked very grave. After a long silence she asked me whether I thought that English would be a difficult language to learn.

I replied that I did not know, since I had never heard anyone talk English.

CHAPTER VIII

My life now began to be entirely different. All the week I worked gaily for that one glorious day on which my lessons took place. I had bought a grammar of the English language, and studied it whenever I could spare a minute. My teacher seemed much pleased with my zeal, but I soon found out that she had made up her mind to give me lessons in more things than English.

One day when I sat with her in her room, that had never lost its charm for me, she asked me quite abruptly why a button was missing from my jacket, and why my nails were always dirty. I felt exceedingly ashamed at the two questions, and stammered some silly reply. At first I thought she did not like me, but she was so sweet during the rest of that lesson that I felt sure she had grown fond of me. When I got home that evening the cook was already in bed. She looked at me in surprise because I did not go to bed at once, as I was in the habit of doing, but took my sewing-basket and searched its contents.

"What are you looking for?" she asked.

"For a pair of scissors."

"What on earth do you want them for now?"

"Oh, only for my nails."

"Which nails?"

But by that time I had discovered what I wanted, and having sat down on the edge of my bed, I started to clean one finger after the other.

"Well," my friend exclaimed, "something has got into your head to be sure."

"Nothing at all—but don't you think my hands are simply horrid?"

"I believe you are really a proud one," she said, and looked at me with great displeasure.

During the time that I took my lessons, Miss Risa de Vall was always zealous to point out to me the many great and little things that make for beauty, order, and usefulness, and never for a moment did she waver in her noble task. Gently, yet sternly, she checked my often wild behaviour, dealing firmly and persistently with whatsoever fault she found with me. After she had known me for about six months she asked me one evening whether I had no other friend besides the cook. I said "No," and then she told me that she had had a young lady as pupil in the town where she used to teach a few years ago. Would I like to write to her and ask her whether she cared to make friends with me? I was, of course, eager to get to know the girl so tenderly spoken of by my beloved mistress, and agreed with all my heart. I wrote to her on the following day, and received an answer by return of post. Her letter was brief, but sweet. When I showed the note to the cook, she said: "That is a real lady, to be sure." I had, of course, no doubt about that. By the flickering light of the candle, I sat down a few days later to write to my new friend, but found it extremely difficult to begin. But after I had managed to start I never stopped until I had filled at least four to six pages. What I wrote about were all things of which I thought constantly, but never confided to anybody—nay, not even to the cook.

During all this time I had heard nothing from my brother, and nobody knew of his whereabouts. One day I got a note from my father in which he told me that he had received a letter from Charlie. He wrote that he was very well off, and made quite a lot of money. When I read that, my heart beat faster. It is true that I never quite believed what he had said to me at our parting; but now I recalled every word of it, and wondered in a vague sense whether he was going to take me to Vienna. I remembered his advice about reading Schiller and Goethe, and felt a little alarmed because I had not yet done so.

"There is no doubt," I said to myself, "that he is moving in society by now, and my utter ignorance of Schiller's dramas would be a source of constant humiliation to him." The fact that he had not written to me since he went away did not surprise me in the least. I thought that he had been obliged to work very hard, and had no time to spare. In order to be prepared for him in case he should really come for me, I made it my serious business to get a book by Schiller. But where was I to get it from? I had no money to spare for books, and could not think of buying one. In the dining-room there was a book-case, but it was always locked up. The books there seemed to be regarded more for an ornament than for use, since nobody ever took one out to read.

But after another five or six months had elapsed, and no further news was heard of my brother, I gradually forgot those glowing pictures of an easy future, and finally thought no more about them.

When I had been at my place for about two years, I happened to make the acquaintance of a young lady whom I met occasionally in the woods when walking with the children. She used to sit down on the bench beside me, and while the children ran about and played among the trees, she would sometimes start a conversation.

"Why do you always stay at the same place?" she asked me one day.

"Where else should I go?"

"I could not answer that question offhand, but a girl like you ought to try what luck she can have in the world."

"What do you mean?"

"What do I mean? I mean that a girl like you ought to have quite a different position from the one you have at present."

"But why do you say a girl like I am?"

"No nonsense, if you please; you must know as well as I do, that you are as clever as you are pretty."

I thought about what my brother had told me, and then looked down at my hands.

"I always thought that I was very silly and very ugly."

"Fiddlesticks! you are neither the one nor the other, and if I were in your place I should go to a town and try to get on."

"To Vienna?"

"No," she said thoughtfully, and then as if a new idea had just occurred to her: "Why don't you go to Buda-Pesth?"

"To Buda-Pesth? But that is in Hungary: what am I to do there?"

"The same thing that you do here, but with this difference, that there you will be regarded as a governess and not as a servant, and you will receive thrice the wages you receive here."

I folded my hands slowly and devoutly as I always did when I was moved by some great emotion. "But," I said at last, "am I ladylike enough for such a situation?"

"Of course; if you were not, do you think that I should advise you to take it?"

As she said this she stood up, and made preparations to go. She held out her hand to me and stroked my cheeks.

"Good-bye then, and think about what I have told you; I am fond of you and should like to see you happy."

After she had gone I repeated her words over and over again. It was chiefly the one sentence that haunted me. "You will be regarded as a governess and not as a servant, and you will receive thrice the wages that you receive here...." Thrice the wages!... I began to reckon in my thoughts. Three times ten shillings make thirty shillings every month ... that would be an enormous sum which I could never want all for myself. No, of course not. But I would send home half of it. My father's letters told me that business was no better, and a little help from somebody would be very convenient.

"Oh, most gracious Lord," I prayed in my heart of hearts, "thirty shillings every month would mean all the world to us."

I got home rather late that evening, and my mistress reproached me gently for not being punctual. For the first time I did not mind what she said. I had intended to tell the cook of my conversation with the girl in the woods, but then I thought it better to keep silence about it, and to wait events. During the following days I looked out eagerly for my new friend; but a fortnight elapsed before I saw her again. I hurried towards her, hardly taking notice of her cheerful salute.

"Where have you been all the time?" I asked.

"I have been busy at home," she replied, looking in astonishment at my face that was flushed with excitement. I tried to control myself and sat down beside her. Although very impatient and very anxious to continue our last conversation, I did not like to start the subject myself. She, however, did not seem to have given it another thought. Not a single word did she say about it.

When at last it grew dark and I knew that I had to start home, I took my courage in my hands, and said with as much indifference as I could assume: "Oh yes, I wanted to tell you that I have thought about everything you told me the last time, and that I shouldn't mind taking your advice and going to Buda-Pesth." I noticed that she was embarrassed, and the next words confirmed my suspicion.

"My dear," she said, "I am truly sorry to have aroused thoughts within you that might endanger the peace of your present life."

All the happiness that I had felt went out of my heart, and with a voice that was almost a sob, I said: "I really don't understand you.... You yourself said—"

"Quite so," she interrupted; "I have told you about things which, however, I regret to have mentioned now that I can see that my mother is perfectly right."

"Your mother ... you told your mother about it?"

"Well, yes, I have often mentioned you to her, and I told her of our last conversation. She thought it very unwise on my part to have made you discontented with the safe peaceful run"—she emphasized "safe"—"of your life."

"I understand. Your mother does not think that I am ladylike, and that it might not be quite safe to assume that I should keep my situation."

But after these weary words the girl put her arms round my neck.

"You little silly," she said, "don't you know that you are far too good to go into a situation at all? But since you happen to be poor and have got to earn your living, it is far better that you should stay at a place like our dear old Krems, where you are less likely to encounter the dangers that lurk for young people in a big city."

I had by now grasped the meaning of her words, and felt greatly moved.

"I understand you, but you need not be afraid.... I am no flirt."

"Hush," she replied in that soft, soothing voice that mothers use when quieting their babies; "I know that; but don't you see that it is hardly ever the flirt, but always the nice decent girl, who is taken in?"

"No, no," I answered blushingly; "I am sure that nothing will happen to me."

After these words my friend held me a little away from her, and gazed into my eyes long and earnestly.

"No, I don't think that anything will happen to you." Then she opened her little hand-bag and took out an envelope, which she pressed into my hands very hurriedly as if she was doing something wrong.

"There," she said, "I have brought it along after all, in case you wanted to go very much." After that she left me quickly, as if afraid that she might regret what she had done. Then I smoothed out the envelope and read the few words:

"Miklosch Sandor, Registry Office, Buda-Pesth."

I called the children together, and went home as if I was in a dream.

CHAPTER IX

The parting from the family in which I had been so kindly treated for more than two years; the parting from the cook, who had been a friend to me in her simple, unspoiled fashion; the parting from my dear teacher, Miss Risa de Vall; and the parting from home—none of them were easy to me. Lightest to bear of all these partings was perhaps the last-named one. My parents had grown so poor during the two years I had been away that I more than ever longed to help them. When they knew what I was about to do, and when I further showed to them the letter from Buda-Pesth confirming my engagement to three children with a salary of thirty-five shillings a month, they, too, thought in their homely way that I had at last made my fortune. Out of the little money I possessed I bought a small trunk, covered with brown, strong canvas, such as are used as hand-bags for travelling. But after I had packed my things, the trunk, small though it was, was only half filled, so few worldly goods could I call my own. That, however, troubled me but little. While I was packing the cheap things, one after the other, into the bag, I was dreaming all the time of thirty-five shillings, and of the wonderful things I could buy with them.

On the very day before my departure a letter arrived from my brother. There had never been an address upon his former letters, but on this occasion there was one. He told us that he was making quite a lot of money, but he did not say how he made it. I was not surprised at this omission, for I simply thought that he had really become an artist, and did not mention his work because he took it for granted that nobody at home would understand it. But I longed to know what he really was—a painter, a sculptor, or a poet. The last thought made me blush with embarrassment and pride. Yes, a poet—that was very likely, since I was writing poems too; but then, of course, my poems would never be as good as his!

The address given in his letter was the name of a café. During the time that I had still to spend at home I thought of my brother, and at last I had such a very bold and daring idea that I was surprised at my own courage. I would go and visit him. On my way to Buda-Pesth I had to pass Vienna, and I determined to break my journey there in order to look him up. I told my mother about it before leaving home the next day, and she thought that he might certainly be very pleased to see me.

I had put on my very best dress for the journey. It was made out of a cheap blue woollen material. To match this dress I had bought a light blue straw hat that had cost two shillings, and I felt convinced that I looked exceptionally smart. My parents went to see me off, and to make it easier for all of us I kept on talking about the thirty-five shillings every month, and about the miraculous things one could do with them. We arrived at the station early, and paced up and down the platform. When the train at last came steaming in, I suppressed my tears as bravely as I could, took my seat by the window of the compartment, and nodded to my people with a smile on my face. A few minutes later the horn was sounded to signal the departure; my father waved his hat to me, my mother wiped her eyes, and I looked quickly away from the window with a sob in my throat that could no longer be suppressed.

The journey to Vienna lasted four hours, during which time I thought much of my brother. I felt absolutely certain that I had gained a great deal during the last two years, and pictured to myself his joy and surprise when he heard that I had also a little knowledge of the English language. When I had travelled about half the journey it occurred to me to write down a few of my poems, and to ask his opinion about them. I found some white paper in my bag, and started at once.

In Vienna I showed my brother's address to a policeman, and begged him to direct me. A little later I walked up and down in front of a café, carrying my trunk in my hands. So far I had not encountered any difficulties, but now I was not quite sure how to proceed. It is true that the most simple thing to do would have been to enter the café, but I did not dare to do so because of all the smartly-dressed people who sat round the gilded tables. Perhaps, I said to myself, he will come out, or, should he be away from home, go in, and then there might be a chance for me to speak to him. However, after a whole hour had passed, and my little trunk had become heavy in my hands, I stepped quite close to one of the tall windows, and looked boldly at the fashionable crowd, hoping to see him seated at one of the gilded tables. But the faces were all strange to me, and making a last desperate appeal to my courage, I had just decided to go in, when I saw a waiter whose gait and carriage seemed familiar to me. He was standing with his back against the window and I could not see his face, but I had the impression that I had met him somewhere before. I stared at him, and had almost forgotten why I was there when a guest seated near the window tapped the table with his spoon, and the waiter, who had aroused my interest, immediately turned round and hurried towards him. I was so surprised that I nearly dropped my trunk. The waiter was my brother. Without hesitating another minute I went in. He caught sight of me directly, and looking round him carefully in order to ascertain whether he was watched or not, told me in a low voice to leave the café at once, and to wait for him at the corner of the street, where he would join me in half an hour. I did as he told me, but while I stood at the corner waiting for him I could hardly get over my surprise. The whole thing seemed to be a dream. I doubted whether I had really seen my brother, and whether it was true that he was only a waiter and not an artist, as I had firmly believed him to be. When the half-hour was over a young man dressed in the height of fashion came up to me. I felt a new surprise; the smart young man was my brother. I thought that he had his day off, and admired the cut and colour of his suit.

"Do you get tipped so well?" I, pursuing my own thoughts, asked him after we had shaken hands.

"Incredible!" he cried scornfully. "How can you be so utterly tactless as to remind me in such a manner of the miserable profession I am in?"

"Why do you call it a miserable profession?"

"Why do I call it a miserable profession?" he repeated very angrily. "Do you really think that I find a great pleasure in hobbling round fellows who are not fit to hold a candle to me?"

"I thought," I remarked, after a little silence, "that you had become an artist."

He laughed so terribly that all the passers-by stopped and looked at us.

"An artist, indeed! That is more than I have ever expected from you. Do you believe that artists drop from heaven during the night?"

"Oh no," I replied hurriedly, in order to appease his temper; "I quite know that it takes many years sometimes before they make a name for themselves."

"Then, if you know it, why do you demand that I should be an artist, when there was never the slightest chance for me to educate myself?"

"No, of course not. What I thought was that by now you might have found out which of your capacities is the most eminent."

"Oh," he answered, with an air of absolute ease and conviction, "there can be little doubt as to the nature of my abilities. It is quite certain that I should have made an excellent painter if I had ever had the chance to learn the different ways of mixing the colours and using the brush; it is also quite certain that I should have become a great composer if I had been able to study music; and it is also beyond all doubt that I should be a pioneer in the field of literature if my profession permitted the depth of thought and feeling that is necessary to write in grand style."

I thought of my own poems, and could not understand him.

"Why can't you feel and think exactly as other people do?" I asked.

"Lord!" he cried, and laughed again as terribly as before, "how can you imagine such a thing? To be locked in between four walls, to have to carry trays, and to bow and scrape all day long! Can't you understand that by leading such a miserable life as mine, the soul degenerates, the brain decays, and the whole being goes down to the level of a working animal?"

He had perfectly convinced me now, and although I said nothing he must have felt his victory. His face grew calm, and pointing at my trunk, he said:

"Then you have at last grasped what I meant at our parting, and have freed yourself from the narrow ways of country life and are willing to look out for a situation here?"

I told him quickly what I was about to do.

"That beats everything," he said, when I had finished. "Have you gone mad?"

"Why should I have gone mad? Didn't you tell me yourself that I must try to get on?"

"Are you really so silly that you do not understand that you have no right whatever to go in for such a situation as you have described to me?"

"What do you mean?"

"Are you really ignorant of the fact," he continued, without paying any attention to my question, "that people like that do not need a servant, but a ladylike person, somebody who knows how to behave, and possesses good manners, and can teach them to the children in her charge? Furthermore, do you not know that you have not a grain of what is called 'polish'?"

I gave a little sob, and after hearing that he continued quickly: "That is, of course, not your fault. Your intercourse with nothing but country-folk cannot have taught you witty, amiable, and smart behaviour; cannot have given you that indefinable something which makes all the difference between an educated and an uneducated person; cannot have imparted that knowledge to you, without which one is nothing, a nobody, a mere cipher?"

I believed every word of it and cried softly.

"What am I to do?" I asked at last.

"If I were in your place I should not travel down to Buda-Pesth, but stay here. I will use whatever influence I have with my friends, and try to find you a situation. Perhaps you could get a post as cashier somewhere in a café."

"No," I said, controlling my tears all in a moment, "I won't do that."

"Why not? They generally make a lot of money, and a good match at the end."

"No," I said again, and shook my head decisively, "I would rather go to Buda-Pesth."

He shrugged his shoulders indifferently.

"He that will not be counselled cannot be helped. What train do you go by?"

"By the evening train at eight o'clock."

"I am sorry to say that I can't see you off then. I have got a *rendezvous* at eight o'clock."

"A randewau?"

"A *rendezvous*," he corrected. "There you are again; you know nothing."

After that statement he pulled out his pocket-book and began to write down something. When he had finished, he tore off the leaf and handed it to me.

"There, I have put down for you the most important of adopted words, which you ought to know because all smart people express themselves nowadays only in adopted words. Good luck and a pleasant journey to you." He held out his hand, which I took mechanically, and when I looked up he had gone.

I inquired for the station, and went the way indicated by a friendly policeman. After I had taken my ticket I got into the train which was standing by the platform, and by the dim light of the compartment I tried to decipher the slip of paper that my brother had given to me. It ran as follows:

Rendezvous	Mélange
Engagement	Carrière
Bureau or Comptoir	Rouge
Pardon	Noir
Toilette	Milieu
Banquet	Manicure

After I had finished reading the paper I folded it up very carefully and put it into my pocket. At the same time the train began to move and started slowly onwards.

CHAPTER X

Mr. Sandor, the owner of the registry-office in Buda-Pesth, had told me in his last letter that he was going to meet me at the station, and asked me to carry a handkerchief in my hand. I had passed a perfectly sleepless night, and when we arrived in Buda-Pesth in the morning I felt quite stiff, and got out from the compartment rather clumsily, with my brown canvas trunk in one hand, and a handkerchief in the other. I looked up and down the platform, and soon observed an elderly gentleman who hurried up to me.

"Have you come from Langenau?"

"Yes," I said, and would have given a world to know what he thought of me.

"Do you want a taxi?" he asked, throwing a quick glance at my trunk.

All the money I possessed did not amount to more than sixpence, and I shook my head violently at his question.

"No, no; I would rather walk."

"Just as you like."

A few minutes later he asked me whether he might be permitted to carry my trunk, but again I shook my head. After rather a long way he stopped at one of the tall, beautiful houses, and I thought it was the house of the family who had engaged me.

"Are we there?" I asked, with my heart beating to my very throat.

"No," he answered smilingly; "here is my own lodging. I have taken you here first so that you can make yourself a little more tidy before you are presented to your new mistress. My wife will certainly be pleased to help you."

He had opened a door and we entered a pretty-looking room. A lady came in. She nodded at me very pleasantly, and Mr. Sandor said something to her in the Hungarian language, which of course I did not understand. After that he turned again to me: "I leave you with my wife now; as soon as you are ready I shall be ready too."

Not until the door had closed behind him, did I understand the ridiculous position I was in. He expected me to change my clothes, never suspecting that they were my best.

"Don't be shy," the lady said; "do just as if you were at home."

But even if I had been really at home, I could not have done much more. I stammered that I did not want to change my dress, but should like to have a clothes-brush, if there was one handy.

"Of course," Mrs. Sandor replied, "here is one;" and with a smile she handed to me the desired brush. I used it with clumsy haste and gave it back.

"Is that really everything?" she asked me in the same pleasant way as before.

"Yes, everything."

After that she called her husband in.

"Ready then?"

"Quite," I replied, and stooping down to lift up my trunk, I said "Good-day" to Mrs. Sandor, and followed her husband out into the street.

We did not go far on this occasion. He stopped at the corner of the road and told me to follow him into the tram-car, a command which I found great difficulty in obeying. However, I got in at last, and Mr. Sandor sat down beside me.

"I dare say," he commenced after a little while, "my letters were quite clear to you, and that you are in no doubt as to your future duties. With regard to your mistress, I do not think that there can be found a more kind and gentle creature, and I am sure that you will feel very comfortable in her house. As far as the three boys are concerned, you will have to find out for yourself the best way to get on with them, and I hope that you will remain there for a long time."

He kept on talking in this strain, and in my heart of hearts I wondered whether I really looked so silly and common a girl as my brother had thought me. The house to which Mr. Sandor took me was a very fine-looking building. There was a broad marble staircase, covered with a costly carpet, which was kept in its place by rods of shining brass. A smart-looking parlour-maid led the way into a roomy hall, bidding us to wait. I put my trunk on the floor, and with my heart beating fast sat down on the edge of a chair. Mr. Sandor seated himself too, but his heart did not seem to beat any faster. We had to wait for rather a long time, and I was almost wishing that we might be left there to wait for ever. But in the very midst of that thought fell the mellowed sound of footsteps, and a lady entered. I felt so embarrassed that I could not speak, and stood up terribly ashamed. But she never looked at me. She spoke to Mr. Sandor in Hungarian, and I grew doubtful whether she knew that there was anyone else in the room. All at once she turned her head and looked at me with searching eyes.

"Are you quite sure that you will like to stay in Buda-Pesth?" she asked me. I did not quite know what she meant and only bowed my head in silence. "I am afraid that you might grow home-sick, and I should so hate to change again."

"No," I said; "I am sure I shall like it very much."

Mr. Sandor then said "Good-morning" to the lady, and as he shook hands with me he begged me not to forget what he had told me. After he had gone, the lady bade me follow her and led the way into a room that was furnished completely in white. A table stood in the centre and around it three boys, whom I guessed to be my charges, were sitting. They got up as we entered and looked rather shyly at me.

"Your new governess," the lady said to the children. "Won't you say 'Good-morning' to her?"

Once alone with the children, my shyness left me. I shook hands with them and asked a few simple questions which they answered in broken German. After I had taken off my things, I busied myself at once in amusing the children, tired though I was. I built houses of paper on the table, and did various little things to help me to gain some courage.

After a few days I grew more reassured, and dropped my shyness even towards the mistress. I could see that she was satisfied with me, and since the children also were very fond of me, I no longer felt afraid of being sent away.

I had plenty to do. To take the children to school and to fetch them back again. Also to take them for walks when the weather was fine enough. The darning and sewing I did when they lay asleep.

Apart from a burning home-sickness that had taken hold of me and tortured me especially in the evenings I felt quite happy there, and no doubt believed that I had found at last what I had been longing for all my life.

There was one thing, however, that darkened the clear horizon of my days: I had not a single decent dress to wear. It would hardly have troubled me, but I knew that my mistress wanted me to be dressed smartly. She had made little remarks sometimes, which, although never addressed directly to me, gave me to understand that she was ashamed for her friends—whose governesses looked so smart that I had mistaken them for mistresses at the beginning—to see me.

One day my mistress came into the nursery, and, looking around somewhat discontentedly, said:

"The children have been invited to tea, but who shall accompany them?"

I looked at her in surprise.

"Why, I, of course."

"Impossible; you can't go there in that blue dress of yours."

I remembered my brother and what he had told me, and started to fret again about being sent away. I had not been there for a whole month, and had not yet received my wages. But my mind was made up that I would buy a dress as soon as I had my money, and I had already looked in all the shop-windows in order to choose one. There were several dresses that I should have liked to buy, but on looking at the price I was so horrified that I avoided the shop-windows for days afterwards.

My shoes were wearing out too, and when the thirty-five shillings at last fell due, there were so many great and little things needed that the wonderful thirty-five shillings melted down to a few small coppers before I had been able to think of buying a new dress.

One evening, when I was busily putting the children to bed, the master came into the nursery and, after having exchanged a few words with each of the boys, stepped over to where I was standing and touching my blouse he said:

"Don't you feel cold in it?"

It was a very simple remark, and quite justified too, because it was cold and the blouse was thin, but the look that he threw at me reminded me of coarse and ugly words I had often heard before.

I said that I did not feel cold, and when he reached out his hand again I stepped back quickly.

He came in earlier from that day onwards, and spent much time in the nursery. He talked chiefly with the children, but all the while his eyes wandered over me, and I felt that each look he gave me was like a new offense. One afternoon when my mistress was out, the children at school, and I was sitting in the nursery busy over some mending, the door opened and the master came in. It was not his wont to leave his office during the daytime, and bowing my head a little I looked at him with some surprise. He closed the door very carefully and leaned against the table. I had taken up my work again, but my fingers trembled. He did not speak, and the silence became unbearable to me.

"Why," he said at last, "why don't you look at me?"

"Because the children need the things," I replied, bending my face still closer over my darning.

"Quite so; but if I want to speak to you, you ought to have a little time."

I thought that I had been rude, perhaps, since after all he was the master, so I got up from the chair and looked at him submissively.

"You know," he said very slowly and with a peculiar inflection in his voice—"you know that I mean to be kind to you, that your welfare interests me, and that I would not mind a little sacrifice on my part if you would only appreciate it."

I opened my mouth to make some clumsy reply, but with his hand he waved to me to be silent, and continued:

"You must know yourself that you are in somewhat pressed circumstances, and I am quite willing to give you a large advance. There is, of course, no need that you should mention that to my wife...." And while he finished the last sentence he produced a small bundle of bank-notes and put it on the table.

At that I lost my head and flew into a terrible rage.

"Take that money away," I shouted, "or I will tear it up!" and because he did not take it away at once, I flung it at his feet. He stooped to pick it up, but his eyes as he turned them to me were shining with anger.

"I am going to tell my wife at once," he said, "to get a lady and no servant-girl for my children."

After that he went.

I was determined to leave the house immediately, and could scarcely wait for the evening when the mistress would come in. But before she came in I received a letter from home that contained most pitiable news about the financial side of their circumstances. "Could not I send a little money, just to keep the little ones from starving?" was their humble yet urgent request. I had received my salary a few days ago and not spent it yet. I took every penny of it and hurried to a post-office. After the receipt was handed to me I felt somewhat relieved, and having hidden it in my pocket very carefully I hastened home.

It was getting late and I started to put the children to bed, inwardly troubled and disturbed because it had occurred to me that I had no money and could not very well leave my place before another month. I would not think of looking out for another situation in Buda-Pesth itself. I had suffered so much from humiliations and home-sickness that I hated the very sight of the houses and streets. I remembered the threat of my master, but it left me cold. If they were really going to send me away it was quite a different thing from casting away the shelter above my head.

My mistress returned with her husband at about eight in the evening. She came into the nursery with her hat and veil on and asked whether the boys had been good. I answered in the affirmative, whereupon she left again. I used to take my supper in the nursery. The dining-room was not far away, and I could hear the clicking of the forks and knives quite plainly. That evening I listened to every sound, anxious to know whether they spoke about me. But they never mentioned my name. My mistress laughed several times, and told her husband about something in her highly-pitched voice. She always talked loudly, and I was constantly afraid that she might wake the children when they lay asleep.

The next morning my mistress treated me quite in the usual manner, and I felt certain that her husband had said nothing against me. After I had taken the children to school I tidied the nursery. When I was about to do the little beds the door opened and the cook came in with a pair of boots in her hands. I had picked up a little Hungarian by now, and could make myself understood quite well. The boots were a pair of mine which I had taken to be repaired a few days before. She told me that the shoemaker was waiting in the kitchen, and named the price that was owing for the mending. With a sudden terror I remembered that I had sent away all my money, and had not a penny left to pay for the shoes. After thinking for a few moments I told her to give him back the shoes.

"But," she insisted, looking down at my feet which were in shoes that certainly were not new, "don't you want them?"

"Oh yes; but what am I to do? If the lady were in I could ask her to advance me a little money."

"What nonsense!" she replied. "It is such a trifle I will let you have the money with pleasure."

I wanted the shoes badly, and felt sincerely grateful for her offer.

"Thank you so much," I said. "You shall have the money back by to-night."

"That is not at all necessary. She does not like to advance us money. I can wait until you get your wages."

When the lady had returned I did not ask her for money as I had intended to do. In addition to the remark that the cook had made about it, I had another reason. I was ashamed to confess that I had sent my last wages home.

During the next few weeks I did something that I have never ceased to regret, and probably never shall. I borrowed more money from the cook. I certainly never asked her for a large sum, but whenever I told her that I was in need of twopence, she insisted on giving me ten shillings, and I spent them as quickly as I received them. In that way I owed her twenty-five shillings before half of the month was over. It did not, however, really trouble me. Twenty-five shillings, I reckoned, still left ten shillings to go home with. However, something happened which altered my position completely.

The lady was going to give an evening entertainment, and had invited about forty people. All sorts of preparations went on all day long, and the evening promised to be a success. As a matter of course, I was excluded from the proud assembly in the drawing-room, and stayed in the nursery as usual. I was sitting on a low chair reading a book, when I suddenly heard very soft footsteps, and looking up I saw the master. Without saying a single word he bent over my chair and, taking my head tightly into both of his hands, he kissed me. After that he released me, and went out as softly and hurriedly as he had come in. My book dropped, giving a low, dull sound as it fell on the carpet, and I sat motionless for a while. Trembling in every limb, I got up at last, and stepping to my little washstand took a brush, and scrubbed my face until the skin was rubbed through and the blood showed. Having done that, I threw myself dressed as I was on my bed, and remained there till long after midnight. What I had felt during those hours was no hatred, no anger, but a great inexpressible grief. I awoke in the morning like one stunned, and did my work mechanically. When I took the children to school I paid little heed to their talk, but tormented my brain to find out how to leave that house at once. I remembered the twenty-five shillings which I owed the cook, and the horrible fact that my wages were not due for a fortnight. If I was going to leave right away the money due to me would not even have covered my debt. Where was I to get the money from that I needed to travel home with? When I thought of my return to my parents a hot wave of shame swept over me. I had dreamed of it often and often—how I would come home some day with many beautiful dresses and costly finery; but as things had now turned out I was no better off than I was when I had left home. After a few minutes' thought, however, I felt less concerned about that, and finally grew utterly indifferent as to my appearance. All I desired was to have enough money to enable me to pay the cook and to travel to Vienna. Once there, perhaps my brother might help me to go home. Yet, much as I reckoned and much as I thought, there was left no other way out except to earn the money wanted—that is to say, to stay for another fortnight at that hated place.

Sick at heart, but calm and composed, I said "Good-morning" to my mistress an hour later. She yawned as she returned my salute, and told me how much she had enjoyed the evening, but that she was feeling tired to-day.

Once during the morning I went into the kitchen to fill a jug with water. The cook and the parlourmaid stood together and whispered to each other. When they saw me they stopped abruptly, and gave me a disdainful look. They had never looked at me like that, and I grew uneasy. After I had filled the jug I went back into my nursery, but the uncomfortable feeling that was roused within me would not be quelled.

When I returned with the children from school that day, the cook informed me that her ladyship wished to see me at once. I wanted to take off the children's coats first, but while I was wrestling with the arm of the youngest she told me to go at once.

With mingled feelings of surprise and anger I obeyed. The door leading to my mistress's room was ajar, and I entered without knocking. As if she had been waiting for me, my mistress stood in the centre of the room, fully erect, her dark eyes flashing at me angrily.

"Must I be told by the servants," she shouted, without returning my salute, "what a miserable creature I have taken into my house?" And getting into a terrible rage, she yelled: "Out of my sight, and do not poison the air here more than you have done already. I give you ten minutes, after that I will throw you down the stairs if you have not disappeared."

I said nothing and asked nothing. I went back into the nursery and packed up the few things that belonged to me. The children were puzzled and picked up what had dropped from my trembling hands. When I had almost finished I stopped and listened. Someone had set up a terrible noise of crying and lamenting in the kitchen, and a few seconds later the cook rushed in.

"My money!" she screamed; "how am I to get my money now?"

"I am sure I don't know," I replied; whereupon she began to howl like a hungry beast, and to run like a madwoman up and down the room. But all at once she grew as quiet as a mouse, and looking up from my trunk I saw my mistress in the room.

"What is the matter?" she asked, without giving me a single look.

The cook explained, and began to howl anew. When she had finished, the lady turned towards me.

"You wretch!" she said; "you miserable wretch! And I have suffered you to sit at my table and breathe the same air with my children for nine months, you dirty, dirty thing! You—"; and then she said something which I do not care to repeat.

I could feel the blood leave my cheeks when I heard the last words, but I set my teeth and did not speak. Without paying any further attention to either the lady or the cook I continued to pack my trunk, and when I had finished I went towards the door. But the lady stopped me.

"The trunk you leave here," she thundered, "and it is to remain until you have paid the cook."

"I have a claim on a fortnight's money," I said; "that she may have, and I will send her the rest as soon as I get a situation."

They began to consider the matter, and I heard the lady say that she would much rather give me the money, in order to enable me to travel home, since she hated to know that I was in Buda-Pesth. The only thing to do was to keep my trunk back. After that talk she turned to me, and threw seventeen shillings on the table.

"There," she said, in a terrible voice, "out with you, but the trunk is to remain here."

I took the money and looked round for the children, but they had left the room. In the kitchen I met the parlourmaid, who had listened the whole time. She opened the front door for me, and mockingly bowed me out. When I had reached the street I ran as fast as I could to the station, inquired for the next train to Vienna, and, two hours later, sat in one of its compartments. Pressing myself hard into a corner, I looked round now and again very shyly and very carefully, because I thought that I had heard someone call: "You wretch! you miserable wretch! You dirty, dirty thing! You—."

I trembled all over with excitement, and closed my eyes; but although utterly sad at heart, I shed no tears that night. We reached Vienna the next morning, and for a few moments I thought of calling upon my brother. But I gave up the idea. Would he not only scorn and despise me? So I travelled on to Langenau. It was dark when the train steamed into the well-known little station, and I hastened home. The children were all fast asleep, but my parents were still up. Both of them were startled to see me, and besieged me with anxious questions. I said that the whole family with whom I had been had died. Later on my father also went to bed, and I was alone with my mother.

"Where is your trunk?" she asked me.

I replied that it was going to be sent on to me.

There was a lengthy pause, during which my mother stared at me thoughtfully.

"I believe you have got no luck," she said at last.

"I am sure I haven't," I said, watching a great black spider that crept slowly along the wooden floor.

I stayed at home now, and as I did not care to meet any of my old acquaintances I never left the house. There was hardly anybody who knew that I had come back. It is true that I longed to see Miss Risa de Vall, but since I had no decent clothes in which to visit her I would not write to her. My mother kept on asking when my trunk would come, and I answered always, "I expect to-morrow."

To my great surprise the trunk really arrived about three weeks after As a matter of course I was very pleased to have my things back, but to what kind circumstances I owed it I never knew. The very first thing I wanted to do now was to obtain a situation. The circumstances of my parents were no better than their letters had led me to expect. The rent especially proved to be a burning and everlasting question. But where was I to take a situation again? At Langenau?—I would not hear of it. At Krems?—that did not suit me either. I decided to write to my brother, and to ask him to find something suitable for me. The letter, however, was never answered, and things grew no better. I earned nothing, and consequently could buy nothing. A new pair of boots was once more a tempting suggestion. Not wishing to lose more time, I had decided to look out for a situation at Krems after all, when the postman called one day and delivered a letter for me. I recognized at once the Hungarian stamp, showing the sloping cross and above it the flying eagle.

But the handwriting did not seem familiar to me, and fearing that I was going to be reminded of my debt to the cook, I opened the letter with some alarm. After I had read it I did not quite know what to think of it. It was written by Mr. Sandor; mentioning nothing about my last place he told me of a situation which he had vacant, and which he thought would suit me excellently. There were only two children—a boy and a girl, aged between three and five years. The wages were the same. My parents tried hard to persuade me to accept the offer at once, but I had my own thoughts about it and could not make up my mind. Another letter, coming from the same place, was handed to me the next day. Mr. Sandor wrote that as the matter was very urgent, would I be good enough to let him know my decision by return of post.

I put all my things together now, and examined them thoroughly. If that blouse, I thought, received a new pair of sleeves it might do quite well at home; and if I sewed a new belt on that skirt, it would not look so bad. I put aside piece after piece, and decided to start with the mending at once; but before I sat down to take up the needle, I wrote to Mr. Sandor that I should certainly feel very pleased to obtain the situation in question.

On the day before my departure I could not stay indoors, but went out. It was evening, and under cover of the growing darkness I visited all the places that I knew so well and loved so dearly. I passed the house which we had inhabited after our very first removal, and looked in at the open gate. The brooklet there flowed through the yard as it had done at the time when I was a little child; but in the corner, where my flowers had closed and opened themselves so generously for me, there stood a kennel, and a large bushy dog darted at me distrustfully. Very sadly I moved on. The church square had not altered. The church stood in its centre, dark and quiet as of old, and opposite to it there loomed up the house of my former friend Leopoldine. All the windows were illuminated, and the whole building suggested comfort and ease. I walked on again down to the very end of the street, leaving behind me all the well-known cottages, together with the dyer's house, until I reached the graveyard. I used to be afraid of that place when I was a child, and always avoided it as much as I could, but to-day my heart was filled with such sadness that all other feelings were overcome by it.

Leaning myself against the low grey wall, my thoughts went on freely. What had life been to me so far? Scorned and avoided ever since I was a child, with nothing for my own but the quiet thoughts and the secret dreams. How different this might have been if "he" had come, my prince out of the fairyland! But he had failed me too.

And as I stood there staring into the darkness above and beyond the graves, I saw a vision—a circle of flames, growing into enormous size, embracing all the world except myself, leaving me outside and alone.

My parents went to see me off again the next day. On this occasion, however, I did not speak, and walked to the station almost reluctantly. When I was seated in the train I neither smiled nor cried, being utterly indifferent. I did not know that fate was ready for me.

CHAPTER XI

Mr. Sandor did not come to meet me this time. He told me in his letter that I would find my way easily now that I knew Buda-Pesth, and, furthermore, the house of the family who had engaged me was situated close to the station. I found it to be exactly as he said; after having crossed the street I reached my destination.

I had grown very indifferent of late, and mounted the broad staircase without the slightest trace of my usual embarrassment and fear.

After I had pressed the button at the door, a maid appeared and asked me whether I was the new hair-dresser. I thought this was owing to my shabby dress, my shabby gloves, and my shoes; so assuming an air of great dignity, I corrected her mistake. She led the way into the hall, and told me to wait. After a little time she came again and ordered me into another room. It had green curtains on the windows, and a green table-cover spread over the table. I expect it was the sight of the green table-cover that reminded me of my mother's former drawing-room. In order to make a good impression, I had held myself very straight and upright on entering the room, but with my thoughts reverting to a time far away, I forgot my purpose and my shoulders shrank a little, as is their wont.

"Are you the new governess?"

A little confused, I took my eyes from the table-cover, nodded "yes" to the question, and then looked directly at the gentleman in front of me.

"You said in your letter that you were twenty-one years of age?"

"Well, yes, I am twenty-one."

"You don't look it."

I told him it was not my fault, and then we smiled at each other.

He asked me a few other questions, and soon afterwards a tall handsome woman entered. She was my mistress, and took me into the nursery. It was early, and the children were not yet dressed; but they looked so sweet in their nightgowns that I liked them at once.

My life again became the same as it had been at my other situation. I occupied myself entirely with the children, played with them, took them out for walks, and later on to school. Our usual walk was along the wide and stately Danube, which represented a magnificent picture with the King's palace and other grand buildings upon its banks. If the weather was not fine, I used to send the children out on the balcony that ran all round the square courtyard at the same height as our apartments. On account of its smoothness it was a wonderful place for mechanical toys, such as engines, motor-cars, and so on.

One afternoon I had sent the children out there again, and promised to join them soon. When, however, I followed, the children had disappeared. I called their names aloud, whereupon they responded at once, but still I did not know where they were.

"Where are you?"

"Here," they repeated, and while I still stood and listened, a door that had not so far interested me opened, and my little girl put out her sweet dark head.

"Here we are!" she said once more; "do come in."

I did not know the people who lived there, but thinking that they were friends of the family I went in.

The room into which the little one had taken me was occupied by a gentleman about thirty years old, who was amusing the children with stamps and pictures. I thought he was alone at home. He saluted me in fluent German, and with more politeness than anyone had ever shown to me.

I controlled my embarrassment, and took the seat he offered me. The children had entered into an argument as to the possible value of foreign stamps, and the owner of the room turned to me in conversation. At first he only spoke commonplaces with a faint touch of irony in his voice, but he grew grave and interested after I had made a few remarks. Then we began a discussion, but how we started upon it I could never remember. Smoking a cigar and leaning back in his chair with easy elegance, he asked:

"Intoxication or regret—which is the greater of the two?... Is it worth the while?..."

I understood only half of what he meant, and answered that I did not know.

Then I told him about my poems, and he listened and smiled, an odd ironical smile that also I could not understand. At last when I departed with the children he asked me what books I was reading.

"None at all," I replied, whereupon he looked surprised.

"May I get you some from the library?"

I thought it was very kind of him, and said that I should be pleased.

A few days later the porter handed me a parcel containing books, and a slip of paper.

"I have chosen the books in a great hurry," he had written, "but trust that you will like them."

As soon as I could find time I opened one of the books. It was a volume of novels by Jacobsen, and one of them was called "Morgan."

I read it all through.... A man—a dreamer, who loves madly a girl to-day and has forgotten her by to-morrow; and round that man there moved pictures full of glowing colour and sparkling light. I liked it, but did not really understand it.

"Have you read some of the books?" my new friend asked me as soon as we met.

"Yes."

"That novel too about Morgan?"

"Yes."

"Did you like it?"

"I don't know."

"One of the most beautiful passages is that in which he walks through the waving corn-field with his young wife."

"Yes, but I believe he must have been a horrible man."

"Why that?"

"So wilful, so restless, so faithless."

He pulled his soft hat over his forehead, gave me a strange look and smiled.

We met almost every day, generally in the morning when I took the children to school and he went to his office. We rode a little way together in the tram-car, then I got out with the children and he went on. During these few minutes we carried on jumpy conversations, based upon an incident, an idea, or a poem of mine. We talked on dispassionately as it seemed, until we stopped abruptly as if afraid that we had said too much.

By-and-by I began to think of him whether I saw him or not; his face, his figure rose like a blazing question from the midst of the strange, wistful dreams that I had dreamt all my life, and something that had lain within me, dull and senseless like a trance, woke, wondered, and trembled into joy.

Once I did not see him for two whole days, and my heart grew so filled with longing that I wrote a letter to him. Not that I wished to see him or anything like it. No. What I put down on the paper were thoughts that had fallen into my soul, rich, like the raindrops that fall down into a field—visions of such rare, exquisite beauty, that I longed to share them with someone.

I was most anxious to see him next day, but did not meet him, nor the next day, nor the next; on the fourth day, at last.... My first impulse was to run and meet him, but it was arrested by a sweet bewilderment that took hold of me whenever I knew him to be near. It seemed as if he wished to hurry on without taking any notice of me, but then he hesitated, stopped, and lifted his hat. I was struck by the strange coolness of his behaviour, and my heart ached within me.

"How is it," I asked him, "that we see so little of each other?"

He drew a deep breath and looked away from me.

"Because it would be very unwise to see more of each other."

"Why?"

He did not answer at once.

"Because," he said at last, "there are wolves in sheep's clothing."

"I don't understand that."

"Don't you?"

"No."

"I want to caution you."

"What of?"

"Of a wolf that runs about in sheep's clothing and whom you trust."

"Whom do you mean?"

"Myself."

The meaning of his words dawned on me at last, but, filled with a happy, deep-felt trust, I shook my head.

"You are no wolf in sheep's clothing."

He drew a deep breath again, just as he had done before, and looked hard in front of him.

"You are mistaken. I am a wolf—a heartless, terrible wolf; one that would never hesitate a second to devour a sheep that comes his way without a shepherd and a hound."

I glanced at him, and it seemed to me that his face looked haggard and worn. I grew very quiet and very sad. The whole world looked dark all at once, and the joyous song that, like a glorious promise, had filled my brain and soul ceased with a dissonance.

But then a minute later it rose again, shy and soft, at first no more than a quiver, but gaining force and power until it grew into a thrill of notes so sweet and persuasive that I could and would not check them.

True that there was something crying within me, but the thing that had rejoiced before was rejoicing still.

"Did you get my letter?" I asked him after a while.

"Yes, and many thanks for it."

"May I write to you again?"

He hesitated.

"May I?" I repeated.

"Yes."

It seemed to be wrung from him.

"And you will write back?"

He hesitated again, much longer than before.

"I hardly think so; I mean to say sometimes, perhaps, but never very much."

"Only sometimes and never very much!"

"Yes; and that only on one condition."

"On what condition?"

"That nobody shall know of our correspondence."

"And why?"

"Because it is best for you."

"Why for me?"

And before he could reply a great anger rose within me.

"You are a coward!"

He shrugged his shoulders.

"If it gives you pleasure to think that, I will certainly not prevent you from doing so; an explanation, however, might be useful to you. It is not on my account that I do not wish to make our correspondence known, but solely for your sake. A single man is free to do as he chooses, he can go and turn a girl's head and nobody will blame him; but you must know that there are different ideas about the conduct of women."

"But I don't care."

"Quite so, but others do care."

"But I don't mind it."

"But I do."

"Then it is for your sake after all?"

"No, for your sake."

He stopped and looked at me with stern, decisive eyes. I felt so low and mean that I was ashamed of myself. What did all of this mean? There stood a man, and I pleaded and begged for permission to write to him. And he would let me, graciously let me, if I was content with his conditions. A wave of bitter anger swept over me. Would he dare to speak like that to another girl? To the daughter of his superior or of his friend? Or what else could it be but that he was ashamed of me—ashamed of the shabby dress I wore and the situation I was in? Quick as lightning a vision rose before me, a row of girls all dressed in costly gowns ... and for the first time I felt envious.... Was he not right after all? What was I? What were my people?... Poor, wretchedly poor!

"Leave me," I said, and the torture that I suffered leapt into my throat; "I will not write to you."

"You can't do that."

My sadness turned into wrath.

"Why can't I?"

"Because you want me."

His eyes had lost their stern expression, without, however, losing their firm, decisive look, and from that look streamed forth a power more irresistible than any I had ever felt. But I was very proud, very strong, very free of will, and would not submit, so I turned my back upon him.

"I hate you!" I said, and went away.

When it was late and dark and the children lay asleep, I sat at the window and looked down the street where hundreds of lamps shed their gloomy light, and countless people streamed gaily to and fro. They looked all so different in appearance and manner, and yet so alike because of the instinct of pleasure that governed them. Their eyes flashed, their cheeks glowed. They all hurried towards the theatre that was close by, and their haste and anticipation vibrated in the air like an electric current. I felt it all and shuddered, and then thought that I saw a monster of gigantic size with a malicious smile on its lips, and a malicious light in its eyes, kicking onward and onward the coil of carriage-horses and people, laughing madly all the while. To get rid of that horrid picture I closed my eyes and thought of home. There the children would be lying asleep. Two or three in each bed, so they would lie ... and mother would be sitting at the table in a cotton-dress that was mended and patched.... I could almost smell the oil of the little lamp and see the red flame trembling behind the crooked screen. And then I saw myself among the children, restless and discontented, full of a vague longing for somebody to whom I could confide all the wonderful thoughts and dreams that I constantly conceived, and to which mother would have responded with a little tortured smile, and father with a shake of his head, had they known, ... and suddenly I was once more bound in the spell of those eyes that had looked at me so calmly and firmly to-day.

"Because you want me," I heard him say again; and the words that had seemed so hard—almost brutal—a few hours ago, had now such a soft, quiet, reassuring touch that I stretched out my arms as if to cling to them.

I had written to him, enclosed my latest poems, and he had asked me in a short note to arrange for a few minutes' quiet talk. I had never yet met him without the children, and the thought of seeing him alone and undisturbed made me tremble with a strange delight. On a very clumsy pretext I asked for an hour off the next day, and arrived punctually. His salute was very polite, his face very grave. "I have only a quarter of an hour to spare," he said, "and must tell you at once what I intended to tell you." His remark that he had no more than fifteen minutes, whilst I had a whole hour at my disposal disappointed me, and I hardly answered his opening remark. He, however, took no notice of my anger and continued: "Many thanks for the letter as well as for the poems, and it is on account of the poems that I wanted to talk to you. You had the kindness to let me read some of your poems before, and I was struck by the talent they revealed to me, but your versification is as bad as your thoughts and feelings are exquisite. There"—he took my letter out of his pocket—"you may see for yourself what I mean."

I looked perplexed at the letter in his hands, but could see nothing, and asked him to make himself understood more clearly. At that request he smiled—not, however, the malicious smile of old—and said:

"The verses lack all shape."

"Shape?" I asked, astonished and a little hurt. "What shape are they to have?"

"Proper shape; the whole versification is wrong. Look here."

After that he began to read aloud and very slowly, making remarks in between the lines—such as: "There is a foot short in that line; and one foot too many in that one; in that other line the time goes too quick, and here again it goes too slow; the proper metre of the whole ought to be something like this." He read the poem over again, but put in the missing feet by syllables of his own invention, and left out what he thought too much. I had never in all my life heard anything like it, and listened to every word most attentively. After the quarter of an hour and a few minutes more had passed we parted, and I walked home filled with new ideas. As soon as I could find time I examined more of my verses and discovered the same unevenness in their construction.

When I met my friend out on the balcony (I am not sure whether accidentally or otherwise) a few days later, he handed me two books, a large one and a small one. "This one here is a grammar of the German language because—"and now he smiled a kind indulgent smile—"you can't spell your own language yet ... and this is a book on the construction of poems. It will tell you more clearly than I am able what you have to do, and what you must not do in writing your poems."

I thanked him very much for the books, but when I looked them through in the evening, I thought the German grammar most tedious, and the book on the "construction of verses" hopelessly unintelligible.

"It is impossible," I said to myself, "to write in accordance with these books; if I had to do it I simply could write no more." I put the books away, and wrote my poems in the same style as before. A whole week passed before I saw my friend again, and he asked me at once how I liked the books. I was rather ashamed to tell the truth about them and answered that they were all right.

"Did you write anything?"

I showed him my last poem. He read it very carefully and then returned it.

"The thoughts expressed in it are beautiful as they are always, and it is such a pity that you don't study the two books a little more."

"How do you know that?"

"Well, I can see it; if you had taken the slightest trouble with them you could not very well have made such great mistakes."

At first I felt ashamed, but then I grew sulky.

"The books are both very silly," I said, "and I do not think that I shall use them."

"Then you mean to remain a nursery-maid all your life?"

I dropped my eyes and was annoyed at the way he spoke to me, but in the evening I studied the books. The theory of poetry I treated with special attention, and after I had acquainted myself a little more closely with its many rules and ways, I found out soon enough what was the matter with my poems. I kept on studying it most diligently, and a few weeks afterwards I wrote a new poem, for which I got much credit from my friend.

"Let me congratulate you on your 'very first' poem," he said.

His praise had made me boundlessly happy and proud. With terrible certainty I had comprehended that I was socially far removed from him; that I could never hold the balance against him; that I was a girl so poor, so meaningless, whose dreams—nay, not even whose boldest dreams—were permitted to soar so high. But it was different now. A feeling of bewildering sweetness told me that this aristocratic man, to my ideas like a foreign bird with glittering wings, had deigned to rest himself in the quiet woodlands of my soul, ready to fly away again as soon as my flowers had faded and my larks had gone away to die. Realizing the last, I felt a bitter pang. No; that mystic stranger who by a sweet whim of fate had, as it were, come to stay with me for a while, must go away no more. No, never. All splendour would vanish, all brightness would fade, and the heart would forget how to sing. All and everything would go with him: that glorious expectation, never owned and all unconscious, telling me softly, softly, a wondrous, wondrous tale; that strange, delightful embarrassment, that at the sight of him had often, often set my feet and heart a-tremble; those waves of infinite tenderness, gushing up suddenly from depths unfathomable—all and everything would go. Something was roused within me, uplifting itself against that desolation, growing and growing until it towered above all anxiety and fear—a new self-consciousness together with a new strength. Thus I commenced to fight the battle that each woman is called upon to fight once at least, and which is more formidable than all the battles of war that have ever been fought by man.

CHAPTER XII

There was, however, no outward manifestation, deep and passionate though that struggle may have been. It is true that we met each other almost every day, but nearly always in the company of the children, and if it happened that we arranged to meet alone, we had never more time to spare than perhaps half an hour. By this time his attitude towards me had entirely changed. The touch of scorn and sarcasm that had confused and irritated me at the beginning of our acquaintance had turned into gravity and thoughtfulness. I on my part displayed much pride and coolness, since his politeness and reserve made me afraid to betray my feelings, which, after all, were not reciprocated. What he really thought of me I never knew. He was always so kind, so concerned, and yet was unmercifully stern and strict whenever my obstinacy revolted against his will.

One day I was with the children on the balcony, and my mistress had also come out for a moment. I sat busy with some mending, when all at once I felt somebody else was present. Without looking up I recognized the voice that I knew so well, and my heart beat faster. I thought that he would come and speak to me. He, however, did not do so, but spoke to my mistress. At that the blood mounted to my cheeks. "The coward," I said to myself; "he does not even dare to speak to me." I trembled with shame and rage, and nothing on earth could have induced me to look up. Their conversation was short and meaningless, and after a little while he prepared to go. He departed with a polite phrase from my mistress, and with a joke from the children; then I heard a door bang, and knew that he had gone.

I felt like crying with anger and sadness. Could it be that such a man was my friend? As soon as I had put the children to bed, I wrote a note asking him to return all my poems and letters, since I wished to discontinue our friendship, which I had only now found out had never been real friendship. I thought he would do at once as I wished, and was surprised not to hear from him. The days passed by, and after a whole week had passed the porter at last handed me a note.

"I should like to speak to you. Pray decide on time and place."

At first I was determined to send no reply whatever, and kept silent for two days; then I could stand it no longer, and wrote saying "when and where."

"What's the meaning of that?" he asked, producing my letter from his pocket; whereupon I began bitterly to reproach him. He did not interrupt me with a single syllable, and so I spoke on and on until I could say no more. "You are a child," he said at last, looking at me half sadly, half amused. His apparent indifference angered me anew.

"Pray," I said with great dignity, "when will you return my letters?"

His eyes blazed all of a sudden and his lips closed tightly.

"Never!"

"But they are my own letters."

"You are mistaken. The letters belong to me."

He had stopped in front of me, and his face wore the grave, decisive look that I knew so well. All my anger melted, and with a little sob I clung to him. He suffered it for a second only, then pulled himself together, and looked at his watch.

"It is time that you should go."

He spoke as coolly and politely as ever, but the look he gave me was a wondrous look, and when I went home, stunned as it were, my heart pondered on a new revelation, half sweetness and half sorrow.

Later on, I also made the acquaintance of his mother. She was such a gentle and ladylike woman that I should have adored her even if she had not been the mother of the man I loved. She spoke to me with great kindness whenever I met her, and told me one day that she had come across a lovely book, which she would be pleased to let me have if I cared for it. A little timid, but all the more determined, I pressed the button at her door next day. A smart-looking parlourmaid ushered me into the drawing-room. There the arrangement of the furniture and other things showed much taste and elegance, and I thought involuntarily of our own poor lodging at home, of the one room, wherein they all ate, slept, and wept together. The sound of footsteps made me forget that doleful picture. My lady smiled at me, asked a few simple questions, and soon we began to talk.

"I am rather ashamed," she said, pulling open a drawer, and taking out some pieces of paper, yellow from age, "but I can't help it. There are lots of things dating even from my girlhood, and I cannot make up my mind to throw them away."

After that she showed me newspaper cuttings of poems, dried flowers, and many other things, which she stroked softly while pointing out to me their value and meaning. When at length I prepared to go, she handed me the book which I had come for; it was a volume of poems by Mirza Schaffy.

That visit did not remain the only one. Many and many a time I sat with her in the cosily black-furnished drawing-room, and when she gazed at me with that singular, ambiguous look of hers, I often felt like burying my head in the dark silk robe on her lap and confiding to her all my sorrow and grief.

One day I received a letter from home, telling me that they were unable to find the money for the rent which fell due on January 1 (that was in a few days), and that all their things would be put out in the street. The letter worried me terribly; I had sent home small and large sums of money during the two years I had been at my post, but just then I did not possess any money worth mentioning. In my imagination I beheld my parents, sisters, and brothers, shelterless, in a dirty, stormy street, and so great was my despair that I cried all night.

In the morning an idea occurred to me that at first I found horrible and shameful. But it came again and again, grew stronger and stronger, and when it was time to take the children to school I hoped most devoutly to see my friend. Nor did I hope in vain.

"I must speak to you," I said, as soon as I caught sight of him.

He looked at me apprehensively.

"I am at your disposal."

"Not now," I answered, glancing at the children; "I must speak to you alone. Can you spare time on Sunday?"

"If there is anything the matter. Why not earlier?"

I felt immensely relieved.

"Then to-day?" I asked.

"Of course, whenever you like."

After that we appointed the time and place, and parted. But scarcely had he gone than I began to regret what I was about to do. The whole thing seemed to me almost madness.

What right had I to ask him for money? I felt so tortured, so miserable, and when the time of our appointment drew near, I decided not to go. Nor did I. Instead, I read that fatal letter over and over again. It was written by my father, and there was one passage that ran: "Mother is worn out with crying and fretting, and is not feeling well of late. What we are to do if we really have to move out into the street, I do not know. They would never take us into the alms-house, because we do not belong to Langenau at all."

I put my face on the table and wept bitterly. All at once I decided to do what I had meant to do, and looked at the clock. It was a whole hour late for the meeting we had arranged, and I could not expect to find him still waiting. Controlling my sorrows as well as I could, I went about my duty. That evening I was alone, my mistress having gone to the theatre, and after I had put the children to bed I grew so terribly anxious again—chiefly about my mother—that I decided to wait no longer. But what could I do? Surely he was not at home; and even if he happened to be in, could I go and ask for him? Though almost certain that it was perfectly useless to look for him, I went out on the balcony and noticed, half-mad with delight, a light burning in a little room situated one floor higher, where he used to develop photographs, to mend watches, and so forth. I walked upstairs, hardly conscious of what I was doing, and knocked at his door as softly as if I did not wish to be heard. He had heard me, however, and called "Come in," whereupon I pushed the door open and entered hesitatingly. Inside the room I pressed myself hard against the wall, and could not speak. He had laid aside his work at once, and looked at me with questioning eyes.

"Will you not speak?" he at length urged softly.

After that I told him my little tale in great haste, though sobs interrupted me. While telling him all, it occurred to me that after knowing my people's history so well he might not wish to be my friend any longer, and I gazed at him anxiously when I had finished. His face, however, relieved my fears. His eyes wore the thoughtful, apprehensive look that I had noticed several times before, and his lips smiled the kind, well-known smile.

"How much do you want?"

"Very, very much," I said blushingly.

"How much?" he urged.

"About a hundred shillings," I confessed, thinking that a hundred shillings was an enormous sum.

He put his hand on the handle of the door, and looked at me entreatingly.

"They might be looking for you, and you must go; the porter will hand you all you want to-morrow."

But I did not go. Pressing myself still harder against the wall, I looked up at him, and my lips trembled as I said:

"Are you cross with me for having asked you?"

"You are a child," he said with great decision; "let me tell you once and for all that I am your friend, to whom you not only *may*, but *must*, confide all your troubles"—his face wore the entreating look again—"but go now please."

I obeyed as if I was in a dream.

The porter handed me an envelope the next morning, and when I tore it open I saw that it contained neatly folded bank-notes.

From that day onward I felt boundlessly grateful towards my friend loved him, if such was possible, more than I had done before, and could hardly control my affection whenever we met. He, however, remained the same.

To him my poems were the sole and constant source of conversation and perfect though I thought them, he was far from being satisfied.

Now and again he would acknowledge the beauty of a thought or verse and the slightest praise from him was sweet reward to me.

There were, of course, still times when our opinions differed, when I grew sulky and obstinate, and even went so far as to behave with the rudeness of a naughty child. But he never lost his composure; it was generally his calmness and silence that made me conscious of my fault, and I never failed to beg his pardon as soon as I had realized that I was in the wrong.

He on his part was always ready to forgive me, and our friendship was established firmly once more.

But in my heart of hearts I was discontented.

"Why," I said to myself, "does he not tell me the one thing that alone is able to make a woman truly happy? Why does he not give me the slightest sign of his love? Or does he not love me?" That question made my limb shake as if I had received a terrible shock, and many times I sat up in my bed at night staring, with my hands crossed tightly in the darkness around me.

Was there, perhaps, another girl of whom he thought, as I thought of him every hour of the day?

I shuddered at the inexpressible loneliness that would fall to my lot if such were the case, recalled every word, every look of his, and lay, testing, weighing, wondering, until all thoughts had merged into confusion and my eyelids closed.

One day we had arranged to meet alone. I was so impatient that I arrived half an hour before the time fixed for the appointment, but he was already waiting for me. Both of us had more time to spare on this day, and I hoped secretly that he might at last speak.

He did speak, but what he said was not what I had expected to hear. He told me of his boyhood, of his more mature years, and of a first love that had left him disappointed with life.

I listened to all without really realizing what he said, my head throbbed, my heart ached, recognizing one wish only.

"There is no need for him to change his manner towards me; all I want him to do is to let me know," said something within me. I stopped and, laying one hand on his arm, looked up at him in anguish.

"Tell me why you do so much for me?"

It seemed that his face grew pale and stern.

"Because I am your friend."

"And is that everything?" I asked again.

"Everything," he replied, shaking my hand off his arm.

After that I remained so still that I thought that I heard the beating of his heart and mine. But all at once a voice roused me, a voice that revealed to me new depths of his soul, a voice composed of torture and pain, which bridged the way back to happiness and joy.

"Do you really want to hear that phrase?" he said. "You are too good for it; I have made a vow never to remember that you are a woman."

I stood in silence by his side. My eyes looked into the far distance and my thoughts measured years to come—years during which we would give each other all the treasures of heart and soul without ever getting any the poorer—years during which neither of us would know the pangs of remorse, the blushing with shame—years during which I would suffer all that a woman may suffer.

"Do you trust me?" he asked.

"Yes," I answered simply; and we grasped each other's hands in silence....

The time that followed now I can never describe. Our meetings, short though they were, were so filled with embarrassed happiness, with timid tenderness, that no colour, no brush, no pen, could ever do them full justice.

But there were hours of quite a different nature too. Hours when strange moods got hold of us—hours when he pulled himself up, just as if to shake off something—hours when his eyes lost their tranquil light, and looked dark and gloomy—hours when the beast was roused within him. Then I felt and understood vaguely the strength of his passion, and grew almost afraid of him. If he forgot his vow for a single moment only, then woe to our friendship and woe to me!

CHAPTER XIII

A whole year passed in this way, and I believe without doubt that I was truly happy. A dull sense of fear, however, had gradually got hold of me. No more did I sit down to my books when the children lay asleep, as my habit had been, but sat crouched in a corner, brooding over thoughts that would be ignored no longer.

"What would be the end of it all?"

I shuddered when I remembered the strange, sad looks he gave me sometimes. Would it be possible to carry our friendship unsullied through the flames of passion? And then the question rose again, which I had believed to have silenced for ever, with many a beautiful phrase—the question of all Philistines!

"Why does he not marry me? Why not?"

On account of my poverty, and my humble station in life! But could such things come into consideration if a man loved a woman truly? And love me he did, or else how could I account for the interest he took in me, and for his ever ready and never failing devotion? I tried to find something similar among the girls I knew. There was, however, nothing similar. Whenever they touched upon matters of the heart, they smiled a cunning little smile that only disgusted me, but never made me any the wiser.

My poems began to be of a meditative, doleful, over-subtle nature, and he, round whose figure revolved all my dreams, my thoughts, my verses, criticized and corrected the lines, that held all the unspeakable woe and longing of my soul, criticized and corrected them with an odd smile on his face sometimes, and with looks grave, sad, far away, at other times. And then there came nights which brought no slumber to me; nights when I lay awake till daybreak, asking myself that one dull, torturing question, over and over again, until at last its answer flashed quick as lightning into my brain....

One day when we met again, he said:

"I am not quite satisfied with your progress."

"What do you mean?"

"Simply that you are treating one subject in your poems over and over again. That is, of course, not in the least surprising, since you limit your experience of people and their ways to one place only."

My heart beat faster, but I succeeded in hiding my emotion, and answered with some hesitation:

"I, too, have thought of that already." And then I added still more hesitatingly: "And I should like to go away."

We looked at each other now and knew that we lied; but the redeeming words that were in heart and throat died away before the feigned indifference on our faces.

"Where to?" he asked at last.

But I shrank back now—the die was about to be cast; all the dog-like attachment and faithfulness of my sex broke loose, all the ardent desire of happiness that had been waiting quietly and submissively for so long stood up, every beat of my heart, every thought of my brain said "No." The minutes passed and I made no answer; testing, like a sounding lead, his looks searched my soul, and all at once I saw how his lips twisted, and there it was again, the old malicious smile that I had grown to hate and fear so much. I never understood it before, but comprehended it now all in a moment. He did not consider me strong enough to part from him; more, he considered no woman strong enough to part from the man she happened to love; nay, more, he despised every woman, every girl that lived, and, knowing that, I knew also, that not even an atom of his soul belonged to me so far, that the battle which I had taken up instinctively, as it were, was not yet by any means won.

"Where to!" he asked again.

With the quick instinct of someone hunted I realized my position, and now I smiled in spite of the tears that sprang up behind my eyelids.

"To England."

"Why to England?"

"Because I speak a little English and should like to know it perfectly."

"Do you know anybody in London?"

"No; that, however, matters little; all that matters is the money for the journey."

After that he grew very grave and was silent for a long while.

"You know," he said at last, "that you have a friend."

A few days after that conversation I fell ill with inflammation of the lungs, and had to spend several weeks in the hospital. At last when I had recovered the doctor told me that I was not strong enough for a situation, but needed careful nursing and entire rest in order to effect a complete recovery.

"Could you not go home for some time?" my mistress asked me.

"Where was my home?" I thought to myself.

But far too proud to tell her, I agreed, and left Buda-Pesth behind me for the second time.

My parents had moved to Vienna in the meantime. They had not told me much about the change, and in my heart of hearts I wondered what the new shop and the new lodging would be like. When I arrived there, however, I became very down-hearted. It was a picture of misery and desolation. The shop was very small and almost empty, and the lodging consisted of a single room that contained nothing but a little iron stove, one or two beds, a table, and a chair. Moreover, being underground, it received but little air and light. My father was alone at home, and after having greeted him I asked for my mother. He told me that she had taken a place as charwoman, and would not be in before eight o'clock in the evening. Without taking off my hat or my jacket, I sat down on one of the beds and listened silently to all that my father said. I had heard the same over and over again, and now I listened to it once more.

"Do you think that you will have room for me?" I asked at last.

"Of course," he replied; "but you will have to sleep in one bed with the children."

"Where are the children?"

"Out making money."

"How?"

"They are selling papers."

"As soon as I feel better I will work too."

"The main point is that you should be well again."

I looked round the small, badly-aired room.

"I am afraid I shall never get well here."

"Since mother is away from home all day long, I am doing the cooking," he said; "and I think a cup of coffee will do you good."

After that he broke some brushwood across his knees, and laid the fire in the stove. But as soon as he had put a match to the stove it began to smoke terribly.

"That's only from the draught," my father said apologetically; "it will soon pass off."

And so it did, but not before the whole room was clouded.

My eyes smarted and my throat felt sore, but I said nothing, and drank the coffee that my father handed me in a cracked cup. I thought of my brother, and could not understand how it was that he gave them no help.

"Where is he?" I asked aloud.

"Who?"

"Charlie."

At that my father grew very sad.

"It is very unfortunate," he replied, "but he has been out of work for sometime."

"Where is he?"

"He is living with us of course."

I looked round the room again, and my father, who guessed my thoughts, shrugged his shoulders.

"It can't be helped; it must do for us."

Later on my mother came in with the children, who, after having sold their papers, had watched for her at the house where she did her work.

When the scanty supper was over, and it grew late, my brother arrived. I was greatly shocked. He had changed completely. His face looked pale and haggard, black circles were around his eyes, his hair hung wildly over his forehead, his figure was lean, and his movements had lost all their former gracefulness.

I controlled as well as I could the effect which this sad sight had produced upon me, and shook hands with him.

"I am afraid," he said, with the same touch of cynicism in his voice which I had noticed whenever he had spoken to me before—"I am afraid that you won't very much enjoy staying with us."

"As soon as I have recovered," I answered, "I will put everything in order."

"Put everything in order," my brother shouted, shaking with laughter; "do you really think that this man"—he pointed to my father—"would ever allow such a thing? Let me tell you that your honourable papa is extremely fond of dirt."

For the second time in my life I saw the vein of wrath swell on my father's forehead.

"Stop it!" he shouted; "do you hear?"

"Yes," my brother replied, and made himself ready to fight.

I sprang to my feet and placed myself with clasped hands before my father.

"Pray do not listen to what he says," I cried between my tears and sobs; "you know that I do not believe a single word of it."

"For your sake," my father replied; then his clenched fists dropped and he left the room hurriedly.

"He is, of course, acting the offended part now," my brother continued in the same scornful way as before, "and I hope for goodness' sake that you will not be influenced by this comedian and feel pity, which would be ill-placed in his case. You have been away these last years and have had no opportunity to get to know him fully. I, however, see through his game, and so will you after you have spent some time at home. At present you may see in me a scoundrel or something near to it, but I can assure you that although circumstances compel me to live under the same roof with these common people, I am still the gentleman that I was before. Schiller says somewhere in his dramas, a jewel remains a jewel even should it happen to get mixed up with dung. As it is, I am a man whom life has cruelly disappointed only because his ideals were too fine and his dreams touched heaven. It is true that I am perhaps one of the most questionable creatures to-day, but wait for half a year, or say a year—my head is filled with ideas which will, when worked out, affect like an explosion our entire code of laws, together with the whole life as we conceive it to-day. Outwardly I am a waiter, a rogue, or whatever you like, but inwardly I am at work on a kingdom for millions of beings who now toil away half-starved in obscurity—and that kingdom of mine holds a crown for everyone."

"It strikes me that you should first have one for yourself," I said.

My brother shrugged his shoulders.

"I can scarcely expect you to understand my point, since you are still too much swallowed up by the mud of your origin, and therefore utterly incapable of following my ideas. The great doctrine of reincarnation is all Greek to you, and you can hardly see that according to its teaching I am your brother only by chance. As little do you dream that most probably I have been a powerful conqueror, or creator of kingdoms, centuries ago. My great hope of being proud of you some day has, alas, proved to be as fictitious as all my other hopes have proved themselves to be, and I must now alone—great men have ever stood alone—carry out my task."

My mother, who most probably was used to such speeches, had gone fast asleep on her chair, and I went out to see what had become of my father. I found him in a dingy-looking, badly-smelling courtyard, and begged him to come in. He went back into the room with me, and no further quarrels ensued that night. Later on my father and my brother prepared to go to sleep on the floor.

I had laid myself down on one of the torn mattresses, and had closed my eyes at once in order to make them believe that I had gone to sleep. As soon, however, as all were silent I sat up and looked round in wild despair. My mother, tired of her daily work, slept soundly, and I listened to her breathing for a while. Then I glanced over to where my brother lay. He looked now even leaner and taller than before, and his face, all unguarded, showed such a strange expression of disappointment, woe, and pain, that for the moment I forgot his vanity, his brutality, his arrogance. A great pity sprang up within me for his early-spoiled youth, his strange, passionate nature lashing him, as it were, never granting him a second's rest nor reconciliation to his fate. He hated my father because he thought that bad management of the business had been the reason for all our misfortune. But he was wrong. I knew for a certainty that my father had given large credit to people who afterwards did not pay, and the natural consequence of it was that he himself became unable to pay for the goods he had received. Besides all that, there were the large number of children and other matters, which would have melted a bigger capital than my father had ever possessed. It is true that one might say there was no need for him to give credit to people who could or would not pay, but he was too generous and too good-hearted to refuse. Being himself a child of the poor, he understood the bitterness of want, and if he had given way too much to such feelings, he had, God knows, not escaped punishment.

I could not for a long time take my eyes from my father and my brother, who now slept so peacefully side by side as if an ill word had never passed between them.

My mother had to leave home very early next morning, and after the poor breakfast was over, my brother seated himself at the table and called my two little brothers to him.

"Come on, you lazy-bones; go and get your books!" he shouted, after which they produced a few dirty books from a corner. My brother then commenced the lesson with them; he was, however, very rude, and boxed their ears for trifling things. Once he gave the youngest a brutal kick, at which I sprang to my feet and, placing myself with clenched fists before him, said:

"Don't you touch him again!"

My brother fell into a terrible rage.

"That's the thanks I get from you, I guess," he roared, "for spoiling my whole career in giving up my time to educate the boys, a thing which it is true you all consider superfluous. Do you believe that I can quietly see them grow up and become such rogues as I have become, only because I have had no education? Where are you, you dogs?" he shouted, turning to the table again.

But while he had been disputing with me the boys had run away.

"There you are," he said to me, "they are no more afraid of the devil than they are of books. Like sire, like son! The boys are not a bit better than their honourable begetter. However, I trust I shall be able to steady them yet, and will see who is the master here."

After he had for a while scolded and reproached me for my incomprehensible shortsightedness in taking the part of these miserable boys, he reached down a shabby felt hat and disappeared.

When he had left my father entered the room; I could see that he tried to avoid the company of my brother as much as possible.

"What are you going to do?" I asked him, because he was putting on a large blue overall.

"I am going to tidy the room, and after that I am going to cook."

He took a broom and began to sweep the floor. I would much rather have done it myself, but the weariness in my knees was so great that I could hardly stand up, so I remained seated on the edge of the bed and watched him silently. After a while I asked him:

"Have you thought over where I shall go to?"

"Well, the best thing for you to do would be to go into the country."

"But that must not come too expensive."

"You might go up to the mill. I saw uncle last week, and they would certainly be pleased to have you there for some time."

My joy was very great. I had not been there for so many years, and the thought of strolling once more through those lovely meadows filled me with delight.

"There is only one thing," my father continued, scratching his head in some embarrassment, "the fare will amount to at least four to five shillings, but I must try and get the money somehow."

"That is not necessary; I have got as much myself."

"Well, then there are no further difficulties, and if you will tell me when you want to go I will write immediately."

I should have liked best to go at once, but since I did not want to arrive there unexpectedly, I decided to stay at home for a week. During that week I suffered terribly. The violent scenes between my father and my brother drove me almost mad with anxiety and fear. I hailed the day of my departure with the greatest joy, and spent five quiet weeks with the very aged relations of my mother.

The pure, lovely air, together with the sunshine and the wonderful tranquillity all around, soon made me feel better, and I was able to walk again without pains in my knees. As soon as I felt better I asked myself: "What now?" The thought of remaining at home was unbearable to me, and yet I considered it to be my duty to stand by my parents in their troubles. I turned the question over and over again in my mind, but much as I thought and much as I reasoned, there was no way out. "I must stay at home," I said to myself, "to work for them, and the sooner I begin the better for us all."

With that resolution I returned to Vienna. The conditions of my parents were, of course, still the same, and I was very anxious to find work in order to contribute to our livelihood. After looking about for some time, I obtained a situation during the afternoons to look after a boy of nine years of age, whose mother had come over from America and intended to stay in Vienna until January.

But bravely as I worked, and much as I tried to feel happy and contented, I was far from being so. The common misery, and more than that the quarrels between my father and my brother which were ever sought for by the latter, affected me greatly, and my scarcely recovered health began to fail again. When I came home in the evening I used to sit down at the small window and stare out in the little courtyard, which was surrounded by a grey, massive wall, at the top of which, looking like a roof, hung a piece of sky.

It happened many times that I still sat there after the courtyard wall and sky had long become invisible, and a single lonesome gas-jet timidly streamed forth its cool, pale, trembling rays through the darkness.

But when I knew myself alone, I burst into tears—into those tears which, in spite of all their bitterness, soothe and relieve.

My mother often looked at me with sorrowful, troubled eyes, but the only answer I made to her silent questions was a woeful little smile.

"What could I have told her?" She did not know that another thing tortured me besides the misery of poverty that we all shared. She did not know him, nor would she have understood it all. So I suffered on, and suffered inexpressibly. Now and again I received a letter from him—cool, formal lines, containing sometimes in a light, casual way the question, "What was I going to do?"

I read these notes a thousand times, hid them away like costly treasures, and reflected in a helpless, stupid manner on the wonderful endurance and submission of a girl's love. And once in the midst of these reflections I remembered suddenly the little story called "Morgan" which he had given me first to read—remembered the man full of restless desire, the dreamer, the idealist, the conqueror, the despiser, who was by the purity and virtue of a woman brought to acknowledge "love" at last. And whilst I yet pondered over it, my heart grew strangely calm.

"Mother," I said the same evening, "would it not be far the best if I went away again? I would, of course, send home my monthly wages, so there would be no difference in the money, and one less to feed."

My mother gave me a quick, uncertain glance, and said in a singular, hesitating manner: "You want to go back to Buda-Pesth, don't you?"

I felt my heart beat to my very throat, but my eyes, as they looked into hers, did not waver. "No," I answered, "I want to go to England."

At first it seemed that she was relieved from some secret fear, then her face looked the same again.

"Yes, it would be far the best," she replied, in the tired, tormented voice of those who had given up all hope.

When everyone had gone to sleep, I sat down to write to my friend. Trembling with excitement and haste, repeating the same thing over and over again, I asked him to send me the money to go to London. His answer arrived two days later—lines so full of tenderness, readiness, and devotion, that the tears thronged into my eyes. "Would I not arrange to see him before I went away?" he asked at the end. But of that I would not think. I knew the charm, the power of his eyes, and trembled for my victory so hardly won.

CHAPTER XIV

London, terrible, magnificent London, to my eyes like a huge monster, moving countless fangs in countless directions. I walked along, stunned, benumbed, dazzled as it were, with neither feeling nor thought, just shrinking a little when I saw the frail figure of a paper-boy slip through the mass of carriages and horses, risking his life a hundred times in order to catch a single copper. And yet, if he had been crushed by the wheels of a motor, or by the hoofs of a horse, would that have mattered? The wave of pleasure and corruption would rush onward, and only in a dingy little room a pale, ragged woman might grow still a shade paler if by the break of dawn her boy had not come home. And realizing that, something within me revolted; I thought of Him in whose honour we are reverently building altars of gold, burning incense, and all at once to me He lost His glory.

Was He not sleeping within a leafy bower, drunk, and forgetful of His World?

And was there nobody who dared to rouse and sober Him?

The next second I was myself again. A silken gown rustled, a silver horn whistled, and people next to me laughed. Feeling very tired and shivering with cold, I longed for shelter and rest. At last, after much asking and useless running here and there, I found a cheap German home for young girls. My limbs were trembling, and I could hardly stand when I was shown into the room of the directress. I remained on the threshold for a few minutes, so sweet and pleasing to me was the sight of that cosily furnished place. All was softness and luxury; a profusion of carpets, cushions, and easy chairs around a sparkling fire. On a little table there was a vase with fresh flowers, and in a cage near by a little yellow bird was swinging to and fro. Next to the fire there sat an elderly lady, with shawls round her shoulders and shawls on her knees. I felt like sitting down, closing my eyes, and saying nothing. However, the lady told me not to sit down because my wet clothes might soil the covers or the cushions. So I remained standing, and answered her questions as precisely as I could.

"Is it a situation you want?"

"Yes."

"And to stay here while you are looking for something suitable?"

"Yes."

"You could hardly have found a better place than our worthy home, but before I regard you as one of its occupants, I must ask you if you have got sufficient money to last you for at least two months, in case you should find no situation before then. Our home is a most respectable home, and I could not think of taking in anybody with a doubtful character."

As my friend had not only sent me enough money for the journey, but also a larger sum for ordinary expenses, I told the directress that my money would last for the board, but in my heart of hearts I was determined not to stay there for two months.

After having settled everything to her satisfaction, she pressed a button, and ordered the entering servant to take me to my room. This time there was no need for me to fear that I might soil any covers or cushions. The room looked cold and grey, and seemed to be as damp and dreary as the foggy streets themselves. It contained a few wardrobes let into the wall, a few washstands, and eight beds.

"Are the beds all occupied?" I asked the maid.

"Of course," she replied, gazing at me with some surprise.

A little later the home filled with girls of all ages, and when the supper-bell rang, the dining-room was crowded with about two hundred girls. After supper, at which the girls were very noisy, we had to go into another room for prayer. On a footstool knelt the directress, with her eyes raised up devoutly to the ceiling. She began to recite a series of prayers, at the end of which we all sang a hymn. Then the directress folded her hands once more, and said:

"O Lord, take care of all the helpless young girls that are in London without shelter and protection" ("And without money," I thought to myself). "Guard their footsteps to prevent them from stumbling, and have mercy on those who have, alas! stumbled already. O most holy Lord, grant our humble prayers, enlighten the blind, and protect the defenceless. Amen."

She looked very sweet and dignified as she knelt there, with her white head bowed reverently, and lost in prayer as it seemed. After a little while she got up and walked out. The girls followed her, laughing and pushing each other; they went up to their bedrooms, and I now became acquainted with the other occupants of my room. I did not care for them. They laughed continually, telling one another shameless stories, and I knew from their conversation that they were mostly chamber-maids and had come from Switzerland.

"Have you only arrived to-day?" someone asked me.

I turned round to the speaker, and saw that she was a girl of my age. Without knowing exactly why, I asked myself whether she was pretty or not, and while I answered her, I thought about the question I had put to myself, and decided at last that she was pretty. She had large bright eyes and auburn hair; her face was well-shaped, yet there was something in it to which I could not get used. What it was, however, I could not tell. She asked me a few other questions, and I inquired whether it was possible for me to find a situation soon.

"What kind of situation do you want?"

"I don't at all mind," I answered.

"As you do not seem to be so very particular, I think you will find one easily."

Later on I noticed that she slept in the bed next to me. I liked her best of all the girls. When she got into bed she rubbed her hands with glycerine, that was all. The others took far more trouble in getting ready for the night. Midst laughing and joking they took off their false plaits, etc., and throwing the things on their beds, they began to dance about on them. At ten o'clock the light had to be put out, but the girls became none the quieter for that. They had so many things to tell each other, and several times, when I was on the point of going off to sleep, their laughter woke me again.

By-and-by, however, the stories grew shorter, their jokes less frequent, and at last they all slept the sound, peaceful sleep of heedlessness. Although the girls had not made a very good impression on me, I was glad to rest my tired limbs, and while I listened to their breathing, my soul filled with almost happy thoughts.

On the following morning we had to assemble again for prayer, and I noticed that they were different from those of the evening before. Each girl having received a Bible, we formed a circle. Then the directress began to read a passage out of the Bible, and we had in our turn to continue.

When it was my turn I read:

"And of the rest of the oil that is in his hand shall the priest put upon the tip of the right ear of him that is to be cleansed, and upon the thumb of his right hand, and upon the great-toe of his right foot, upon the blood of the trespass offering."

At the end the directress again prayed for the "poor helpless girls," and after that we were free for the day. As soon as I had got up from my knees, I went over to the directress and asked her to give me an address at which I might inquire for a situation. She motioned me to follow her. In her room she sat down, and looked at me thoughtfully.

"You want to look for a place already to-day, don't you?" she said. "I can quite understand that you are in some hurry; but, as I have agreed to take care of your soul, I cannot let such an earnest matter as this one pass without giving you a little motherly advice. So many girls arrive in London daily, who have left their homes in the sweetness and innocence of their youth, and who return home quite otherwise. Therefore I should like to know that you are prepared for all dangers which might threaten you. Will you promise to pray to God to take care of you, to assist you, to counsel you, to lead you?"

I promised everything.

"There, then, are several addresses where you may try to find something suitable, and I only hope that you will be received into the bosom of a God-fearing family."

I thanked her very much for the slip of paper she had handed me, and, after I had left her, I sprang upstairs to get my hat and coat. Several of the girls were just putting on their hats, and asked me where I was going to. I told them, whereupon they replied that they wanted to go to the same place, and that I might come with them because they knew the way. Although I felt sincerely grateful for their offer, I was annoyed at the time they took to put on their hats. There was only one looking-glass in the room, and this the girls surrounded, adjusting their hats by the aid of hat-pins, of which they possessed incredible numbers. Whenever I thought that they had at last finished, they took off their hats again, declaring that they did not look their best to-day, and tried all means and ways to look it after all. I stood there waiting for them with my quiet little hat on my head and felt terribly impatient. I longed to find a situation in order to be able to leave the home. The others, it is true, did not seem to have a similar wish. Apparently they were quite contented, even happy, and cared little whether they got a situation or not. A fair girl who was so tall that she towered above the others had given a bold sweep to her great black transparent hat, and was now trying it on.

"Do you find it becoming like that?" she asked, after which she had to turn round and round, and was assured eventually that it was very becoming.

Just when I thought that she looked horrid, she turned to me and said:

"Hurry up, little one; we are almost ready."

"I have been ready for a long time," I answered in surprise.

But now it was her turn to be surprised.

"Surely you don't mean to go out like that?"

"Well, of course."

At that they all laughed, and, after having cooled down a little, one of the girls said:

"You don't seem to know London ways yet, and we shall have to do a little for you. In such clothes you will never get a situation; I can give you that by writing, my dear."

"But what am I to do?"

"Leave her alone," the fair girl intervened; "she who does not possess chic by nature will never acquire it."

The others seemed to agree with this, and said no more about me. When all of them had their hats on, they began to hunt in their trunks and bags for such things as a pair of gloves without holes, a handkerchief that was clean, and so forth.

At last they were ready to go, and I kept behind them in the street because I thought they were ashamed of me. The remark, however, that one of the girls had made—namely, "that she could give it to me by writing," that I would never find a post in such clothes—haunted and troubled me.

It was most important for me to find a situation as soon as possible if I did not want to ask for more money from my friend. And that I would not do. I had sent him a few cards during the journey, but was going to write him a long letter as soon as I knew how matters stood; and so full was I with that one thought that to-day I cared little for what went on around me. Only once when we went over a mighty bridge did I stop, and look enraptured at a swarm of greyish birds such as I had never seen before. They were sea-gulls.

After much wandering which made me very tired and recalled to my memory the old pains in my knees, the girls stopped at last in front of a beautiful house and entered gaily. I followed them into a large room, and on the benches and chairs there sat girls who apparently were also looking for situations. At a writing-desk an elderly lady and a young girl were sitting and writing diligently in large books which were placed in front of them.

The girls were called up one after the other, and after those who had been there when we arrived had gone, it was our turn.

The tall, fair girl went up first and sat down with affected dignity.

"What I want," she said to the inquiry of the elder lady, "Is a place where I should get enough spare-time to see my friends at and away from home; also I do not wish to have charge of more than one child, not older than twelve, and not younger than six years."

The younger lady at the desk put down the notes; but the elder one smiled politely, and said she was sorry, but there was nothing suitable at present. Shrugging her shoulders, my fair friend left the chair, and another of the girls explained what she wished to get, and what she did not wish to take. But she, too, was sent away with a polite phrase only. After they were all told that nothing suitable was to be had at present, they prepared to go, and went away together without giving me another look. I felt greatly relieved when they had gone; and because it was now my turn I stepped near the desk.

"I expect you have only just arrived."

"Yesterday."

"I am afraid you had a bad crossing, you look so pale."

I told her that I was always pale.

"What are your requirements?"

"I have no requirements whatever—all I want is a situation."

"Have you got any papers?"

I handed her my reference from Buda-Pesth, and, after having read it carefully, she folded it up and looked at me thoughtfully.

"Would you mind doing housework?"

"Not at all," I replied, full of new hopes.

She reached for one of the large books, and turned the leaves over.

"Would you like to go in the country?"

"With all my heart."

At that she nodded eagerly, and pointing with her finger at a place in the book, she said:

"There is something which I am sure that you would like. The lady here is trying to find a girl who speaks German and who would not object to do the work in the house, besides being a companion to her daughter aged fourteen. There is also a young French woman who is to help you. What do you say to it?"

I thought of the eight beds as well as the girls in the home, and said that I should feel very happy if I could obtain that situation.

"The lady is coming again at two o'clock, and if you like you may wait here and speak with her."

Controlling my joy as well as I could, I decided to wait, and sat down on my chair again.

The lady arrived in about an hour. She looked nearly forty years of age, and was very kind. She only repeated what I had heard already, and I agreed to everything. Finally she gave me a card with her name and address upon it, and told me to start two days later. When everything was settled she held out her hand to me, but took it back again as if she had thought of something.

"Have you had your dinner?"

"No," I said truthfully.

"Then you must come with me."

She made me sit down in the carriage in which she had come, and a little later we were seated round a table.

"What would you like to eat?" she asked me.

I said it was all the same to me, whereupon she ordered a lovely dinner and looked much pleased that I liked it. When I had finished she took me into the street again and looked round for one of the red motor-buses. She soon spied one and begged the conductor to take care of me, and to tell me when I had to get out. Then she nodded to me once more and I rode back to the home. As soon as I got there I went to the directress and reported my good luck. She, however, looked a little doubtful.

"The whole matter is somewhat suspicious," she said; "it has gone too quick, but all that we can do is to trust in Him."

I assured her that I did so, and then I went up into the bedroom and wrote to my friend a letter of some length. The girls who had left the home with me in the morning returned towards supper-time and inquired a little scornfully whether I had got a situation. After I had told them of my success they looked greatly surprised and asked me to tell them all about it. I told them all I knew, and after I had finished the tall, fair girl again shrugged her shoulders.

"That is only the place of a kitchen-maid, but for doing the cooking and scrubbing the floors I am too good, I think;" and while she said that she turned her hat into another shape.

CHAPTER XV

The little place where my mistress lived is situated on the Thames, about two hours' journey from London. The lady herself came to meet me at the station. The house to which she took me stood somewhat back from the others, near to the bank of the river. Talking kindly all the while, my new mistress showed me into a large pleasant room, and told me that this was to be my room. Left alone, I looked round. The low walls were covered with a pretty light-grey paper, and the black massive iron bedstead had a cover of similar colour. In one corner there was a washstand with a grey veined marble slab, and white china standing upon it. On the right, a chair and a table. The room had two windows, one of which faced the courtyard. The view, however, was barred by the protruding roof of a shed, overgrown so thickly with creepers that it looked like underbrush in the woods. That roof I grew to love immensely, and, later on, I watched with keen delight how its colour changed from the most tender green of spring to the burning red of autumn. The second window gave me a view of the garden which was sloping down to the river, and on the other bank I could see extensive meadows of a most exquisite green. It was this window at which I leaned and looked out, after I had, with a deep breath of relief, noticed the cleanliness and comfort of the room.

I looked down at the Thames, of which I had heard so often at school, and for which I received so much scolding and thrashing because it was so hard to remember whether London or Paris flourished on its banks. I looked down on the meadows lying soft and dreamy, untouched by the hand of greed. No tree, no bush, as far as the eyes could wander, nothing but the free, lovely fields, impressing one with a sense of prosperity and peace. To me that peace and stillness was so pleasing that I folded my hands involuntarily.

"Life," I said in a low voice, "wonderful life!" for wonderful I thought it, in spite of the weariness in all my limbs and the ardent longing in my heart.

I was called down a little later and made the acquaintance of the daughter and the French girl. The former spoke German, the latter did not. As I myself did not understand French, my fellow-servant and I spoke

English, and spoke it badly. I found out very soon that she was a most superficial girl who hated thoroughly the work we had to do together in the rooms and kitchen. Though she was only seventeen years old she had already flirted a good deal, and whenever we were at work beating the carpets, washing up the dishes, or cleaning the boots and clothes, she told me of the men who had crossed her way and been more or less fatal in her life. After having detailed also the latest of her conquests, a grocer or a chemist's apprentice, she urged me to tell her something about myself. But at that I shook my head decidedly and smiled. What could I have told her? That what made me sometimes so happy and sometimes so sad was a fairy-tale of such wonderful delicacy that she could never have understood it. And when, regardless of my smile and silence, she dived again into the waves of her adventures, I was all the more quiet and worked twice as quickly as she did.

So time passed away painfully, yet mingled with the blissful hope that he would come for me some day; unconscious, but not to be shaken, it lived within me, and innumerable times I pictured to myself how it would happen. The bell would ring a short, energetic ring, and he would stand in the kitchen all unexpected and all unannounced. Then I would take him upstairs to my room, show him happily—like a child shows his toys—the little forest below my window, the river and the green fields beyond it, until suddenly he would notice my black dress, my white apron, and the flowing bonnet-strings—badges of my position—would comprehend the endurance of my heart, my hands, and silently take me in his arms.

These dreams, however, were the most foolish dreams that I have ever dreamt.

By-and-by I learned to know thoroughly the ways of English home-life. Although my mistress was a widow, she gave all sorts of entertainments characteristic of English people, such as tea-parties, picnics, and so forth. It is true that these large and small gatherings doubled my work in every respect, but I tried to compensate myself by catching now and again an English word, in order to enlarge my knowledge of that language, which was poor indeed, since my mistress as well as her daughter generally spoke either French or German. Yet, with much zeal and diligence (I studied in English books deep into the night) I progressed very nicely.

My mistress always treated me most kindly, but I could not help smiling sometimes at the relations between her and her daughter. The fifteen-year-old girl tyrannized over her mother in a most incredible way. Unfortunately my mistress was convinced that her darling possessed everything that was needed to make a great artist, and did all in her power to develop the talents of that future genius. It is true that the girl sang, danced, painted, and wrote poetry, but I am doubtful as to the merit of her accomplishments. One day, when I was busily beating the carpets, my mistress rushed out of her room, and looking pale with nervousness she begged me to stop that noise because Miss Daisy was about to write a poem. I lifted the heavy carpet down at once, but thought of my own poems, which still proved to be a secret source of my scanty joys, and asked myself how many poems I could have written if absolute stillness was necessary for the writing of them.

They were composed while I was working, while I was running up and downstairs, and there was nobody who cared. Nobody? No. Now and again a letter told me that the one or the other of my poems was exceptionally beautiful.

When I had been at my post for some time, a great change happened. Miss Daisy fell ill with scarlet fever. As soon as the French girl knew about it she left the house.

"Do you want to leave too?" my mistress asked me.

"Certainly not," I replied.

After seven weeks full of anxiety and fear, the doctor ordered the patient a change of air. All the necessary things were packed up immediately, and a few days later we looked out on the northern sea. I had got a room to myself, and was impatient to retire there. The evening came at last, but tired though I was, I did not think of sleep. I stepped to the window, opened it as much as one can open a window in England, and gazed enraptured at the heaving waters, on which the moonlight glittered and danced. It was very late before I went to bed on that night, and very early when I got up next morning. Nobody was astir yet, and I dressed noiselessly. During the night I had had a strange dream and felt like writing it down. I looked for a sheet of paper and while the sky deepened from pink into red, I wrote a new poem, and entitled it "Ruby."

After we had stayed at the seaside for about five weeks we returned home, and my mistress did not engage a second servant for the present. My duties increased and I had less time to spare than before, but still filled the few moments of leisure I could find with the study of the English language.

One day I came across a book by Milton, and in spite of my defective knowledge of the language, read most eagerly his "Paradise Lost," and was overwhelmed by the picturesque language and by the bold imagination and grandeur of the whole. Many, many times, also, I looked up the page on which was written:

"When I consider how my light is spent
Ere half my days, in this dark world and wide,
And that one talent which is death to hide,
Lodged with me useless, though my soul more bent
To serve therewith my Maker, and present
My true account, lest He, returning, chide;
'Doth God exact day-labour, light denied?'
I fondly ask: but Patience, to prevent
That murmur, soon replies: 'God doth not need
Either man's work, or His own gifts; who best
Bear His mild yoke, they serve Him best; His state
Is kingly: thousands at His bidding speed,
And post o'er land and ocean without rest;
They also serve who only stand and wait.'"

And each time that I read that poem I fell into a strange brooding mood. A mood from which later on sprang my greatest defeat and my greatest conquest. By-and-by I bought the poems of Lord Byron, Keats, and also of Longfellow, and not a single day passed without my being able to do a little reading. That does not mean, however, that I read all the poems contained in a book. Far from it. When I bought a new book I used to turn over the leaves until I found a poem which I liked very much, and that one poem I kept reading over and over again. It happened also that I used to read a poem on account of one passage only. There is, for example, one poem by Lord Byron, commencing thus:

"Ah! Love was never yet without
The pang, the agony, the doubt."

And a few lines further:

"That love has arrows, well I knew;
Alas, I find them poisoned too."

For the sake of these last lines, I wandered through the whole poem again and again although I did not care for the rest.

My favourite poem by Keats was:

"I had a dove, and the sweet dove died,
And I have thought it died of grieving.
Oh, what could it grieve for? Its feet were tied

With a silken thread of my own hands' weaving.
Sweet little red feet! why should you die?
Why should you leave me, sweet bird! why?
You lived alone in the forest-tree;
Why, pretty thing, would you not live with me?
I kissed you oft and gave you white peas;
Why not live sweetly as in the green trees?"

This poem seemed to me so simple, so sweet, that I recited it while I did the washing or cleaned the floor. It is a habit of mine to recite a poem whenever my occupation permits it; the even movement of a verse produces a most soothing effect on me, and I know of no other thing in existence holding so much grace and sweetness as the symmetrical flow of poetry. In this quiet manner, time slipped away. During the first month of my stay in England my friend had written to me often, but little by little his letters became rare; sometimes he kept me waiting for months, and then I thought that he had forgotten me. At such hours my longing for him was beyond all telling; how I watched for him and waited, expecting vaguely that something unaccountable, something wonderful would happen to bring him to me; and so firmly did I believe this, that I began to tremble each time the bell was rung, thinking that he had come. But he never came.

One day my mistress told me that she had received an invitation to go to Scotland, but could not take me with her.

"I think," she said, "as you have not seen much of London yet, you might like to become better acquainted with the town. So the best thing for you would be to stay at the home for a few weeks."

"I don't think I should like to stay at the home," I replied.

"Why not? That home is a very worthy home indeed, and I feel sure that you will be well cared for."

After that I did not dare to say more.

CHAPTER XVI

The preparation for the departure began at once. The next day my mistress took me to the home herself, commended me to the special care of the directress, and I lived once more in the room containing the eight beds. I knew none of the girls and was not at all eager to know them. However, when I entered the dining-room in the evening I had a surprise. Somebody called my name. I was much astonished, and asked myself which of the girls could know me. The one who had called my name was sitting at the table beckoning to me with both of her hands.

"Do come," she said vivaciously.

I did not remember that I had ever seen her, and believed already that she was mistaking me for somebody else, when suddenly it came into my mind who she was. She was the girl who had slept next to me during my first stay at the home—the girl with the large, bright eyes and the auburn hair. I was now glad after all that somebody knew and greeted me.

"Are you looking out for a situation?" I asked her during supper.

"No," she replied, "I am living here"; and then she told me that she was a correspondent for German. I listened and shook my head.

"I cannot understand how you can put up with it—to stay here for good."

"Why?" she asked.

"Well, on account of the sleeping."

"I am used to it."

"I could never get used to that."

"In this world," she replied, "one has to put up with lots of things." And while she said that, her face grew very sad. When the bell rang for prayers we stood together, and when the hymn was sung I listened to the soft melancholy note that trembled in the girl's voice. The next morning I decided to go to the British Museum, since they all told me "everyone ought to see that."

It was only a few minutes' walk from the home, so I did not have to make many inquiries about the way. When I arrived at the entrance I was charmed with the countless pigeons, which seemed to be quite tame and fearless, even taking food out of the people's hands. I should have loved to remain there and watch the sweet, graceful birds, but there was something within that reproached me for my indifference towards the treasures of the British Museum itself. In order to quiet that something, I at last mounted the steps leading to the different rooms. I am sorry to say that my knowledge is far too small to appreciate the treasures accumulated in these rooms. I remember innumerable things, black from age, lying behind glass cases; their meaning and value, however, I did not understand. When I entered the room with the Egyptian mummies I felt the same reverence that I felt as a child on entering a church, and I only dared to walk about on tip-toe. That respect passed, however, the longer I gazed at the dark, lean faces, and finally they seemed to me to be no more than large babies put in swaddling clothes. There in front of me, a glass case held the last remains of a King—a hand adorned with yellow rings. Once upon a time that same hand had moved imperiously, and a thousand slaves had trembled at the sign. "Where is thy country to-day—where thy army, and where art thou thyself, oh mighty King? And what, oh tell me, became of all thy agonies, and what became of all thy joys?" Thus I questioned the dark hand with its yellow rings, and the reply I found was a conviction new to me. That there does not exist a real self—that God has not finished His creation yet—that we are the means towards an object, but not the object itself.

After much wandering to and fro, I arrived at a room that also contained glass cases, to which large and small pieces of brown paper were carefully pinned. At first I looked at them with wondering curiosity, but next minute I was overcome with awe. The brown pieces of paper were papyrus, which I had often heard of, but never seen. There were several of them, but I returned again and again to the one above which stood the following inscription: "Papyrus with five verses of an ode by Sappho to her brother Charaxus."

I could not turn my eyes away from it, and thus it happened that I went to the British Museum every day for the three weeks, in order to see the pigeons and the papyrus. I had an idea in my head of stealing the papyrus, but failed to accomplish that noble purpose owing to two policemen who were stationed close by, and who began to watch me suspiciously. Although the papyrus has, as I can see, not yet lost its old attraction, I must not forget to mention my visit to the famous "Tower." There, however, I did not care very much for the splendid armour which decorated the walls, nor for the large diamond in the jewel-room, round which the public crowded. I left rather quickly the narrow corridors, together with the gloomy rooms, and sat down on a bench in the court-yard, contemplating with melancholy feelings the bright brass plate in front of me, which stated that two young beautiful queens had been beheaded on that spot. The sunburnt leaves of autumn danced over it to-day.

I returned to the home rather late from such excursions, expected most impatiently by the girl who had attached herself to me more and more closely. By-and-by a friendship sprang up between us, the cause of which I could never explain. I think it was her eyes, which at times looked so strangely sad, that had attracted me, and although she had never confided in me, I felt sure that she was troubled by some secret sorrow. One day when we sat together and chatted, a letter from my friend was handed to me. I had been expecting it for a long while, and was very pleased with it. He wrote that he worked until midnight every day, and begged me to forgive his silence. He would write more fully as soon as he could spare time. My friend noticed how happy the few lines had made me, and smilingly she asked me whether that letter was from someone for whom I cared very much, and was that someone perhaps a man? I hesitated a little, and then told her about him. While I did so, she grew more and more sad, and at last she cried.

"I wish," she said, "I had known you before I went to Paris."

At that I felt much consternation, and could not understand her.

"Why," I asked at last, "did you have so little companionship there?"

"No, no," she said, springing to her feet, "too much—far too much."

Before I had understood what she meant, the door opened and some of the girls entered. We therefore began to talk about indifferent matters, but I could see that my friend was not at her ease. Her cheeks were very pale, and her smile affected. A few days later I received a note from my mistress telling me that she was coming back in a week's time, and that she wanted me to leave the home. This was very bad news for my friend; she kept with me constantly, and declared that she would not know what to do when I had gone. On the day before my departure she was again strangely moved, and often began sentences without finishing them.

"Is there anything that troubles you?" I asked her.

"Yes."

"Then will you not tell me?" I said, caressing her hand.

"Yes," she replied, in a voice more agonized than any I had ever heard. Then she closed her large, bright eyes, and, as if afraid to hear her own words, she told me in a whisper something that was very sad.

After she had finished we both cried.

"Is the child a girl or a boy?" I asked at last.

"A girl," she replied tonelessly.

"And is it living?"

"I don't know."

I jumped from my bed and looked at her incredulously.

"How is that possible? Don't you know whether your child is living or not?"

She stared at me with a stupid, helpless look, and my pity was aroused.

"Tell me everything," I pleaded softly: "perhaps it will take a load from your heart."

After that she told me everything. How the man had neglected and abandoned her, how she had faced hunger for nine months to keep her baby with her, how she had fallen ill at last, and was compelled to separate from the child in order to save it from starvation. While she told me all this, her tears flowed incessantly, and I stroked her hands.

"To whom did you give your baby?" I asked in a low voice.

She closed her eyes again as if recollecting something, and said:

"In Paris there is a place where one may leave a child without being obliged to tell one's name."

"And there?..."

She nodded, and leant wearily on the bed.

"But you must have been mad—now you can't recognize your child again."

"Oh yes," she replied, shaking her head violently, "I can recognize it again; each of the children receives a ring of thin metal round its wrists, and on the ring there is a number."

I was silent, and we went down because the bell had rung for supper. We both ate very little, and when the hymn was sung later, I heard nothing but the soft, melancholy note that trembled in the girl's voice. During the whole evening we said no more about the matter. I busied myself with packing up, and went to bed very late. For a long while, however, I could not go to sleep. Several times I sat up in my bed and glanced at my friend. She was lying quite still, and I believe she was asleep. At last my eyes closed too, and half awake and half asleep, I imagined that I saw a little girl who played in a dingy yard; she had the same large, bright eyes, and the same mass of auburn hair as my friend, only round its wrist there shone a small ring of metal, and on the ring a number was hanging.

CHAPTER XVII

My way of living became the same again. Now as before I scrubbed the floor, washed the linen, and looked after the kitchen. Many times during my work I thought of my friend in London and secretly wished to be near her. There was one reason, however, why I could not really leave Marlow. It was this: that I was determined to return the money which I owed to my friend in Buda-Pesth; that was, of course, not easy for me, since my wages were only thirty shillings a month, and out of them I used also to help my parents. It is true that I had sent home less of late, because the conditions at home had gradually become more satisfactory, and my brother had also gone away. My parents had not heard from him for a long time. All they knew was that he had given up entirely the hated profession of a waiter, and gone over seas to try his luck in another land. In one of his more recent letters my father had told me that he had received a newspaper from Brazil, containing the news of a most daring flight made by an aviator named "Aranga."

Underneath this account, however, the following words were written in pencil, "Much love to all of you. I shall be all right as long as my spine is not broken."

To the above-mentioned purpose I now put away every farthing that I could save out of the thirty shillings, and the mere thought of sending my friend the amount of my debt made me exceedingly happy. Now to leave my situation and find another one in London would have certainly cost me money, and to spend even a single penny would have been unbearable to me. About that, however, I made no mention to my friend, but told him only of my occupation and so forth. His letters became very rare indeed, and of late contained nothing but reproaches at my apparent "waste of time."

"Have you," he asked, "gone over to England in order to learn how to cook? There was indeed no need for you to go to London just for that. You know how much I want to help on your education, and to develop your talent. Pray do not insist on sacrificing all your time to others. Try at least to find an engagement for the mornings somewhere in London, and study in the afternoons. I would, of course, support you in whatever way you require."

Tempting though such an offer may have been, I could not make up my mind to accept it, and so I returned with a sigh to my pots and pans. But in my heart of hearts I felt like the little boy in the story, who was for ever wishing that something might come along that would take him somewhere else. However, nothing came. One month passed after the other, and sometimes my feet felt very tired. By-and-by my heart grew weary too, and finally refused to tremble whenever the bell was rung; no longer did I fear, hope, and believe that he had come at last. But I was still waiting, waiting at the threshold of his soul, waiting for the wonderful moment when it would open, and he would step out to me with kindness on his lips and fulfilment in his eyes. Sometimes again there were hours when I almost regretted—hours when my most secret thoughts seemed to come to life and confront me with malicious-looking faces. "Why did you go away from him?" they would ask scornfully. Yes, why had I gone away from him? To get to know different people and different places? Of course, did not he himself wish it thus? Did not I myself want it thus? Want it thus? And after every drop of blood within me had set its "No" against that question, the scornful voices rose again: "And if you did not want to go away why, then, did you go?" And all at once I knew it, and my cheeks flushed with an unaccustomed glow, and my heart was filled with an unaccustomed sorrow. Thus disputing with myself, time passed on.

It happened one night, when I could not go to sleep though I had worked hard all day long, that I lay awake in bed, and thought and thought until all good and evil spirits had gathered around me. Like so many hands they reached down into my thoughts, tugging, pulling, and tearing them about, and when they had gone, there were red letters floating about in the darkness of the room, forming themselves to a question at the end, and the question was:

"May I come back again?"

"Why not?" I said, shaking my fists towards the glowing signs; "is not our friendship so pure, so marvellously wonderful?" ... At that a wreath of flames encircled every letter, and when I read again I trembled.

"That is just why," it said; and behind the letters there rose up a beautiful, transparent light. But I would neither see the light nor the writing, and closed my eyes like an obstinate child. Other nights followed similar to that one, and by-and-by all things seemed to enter into conspiracy against me. My own self seemed to hate and persecute me—seemed to wrestle from me the last faint hope, which I would not surrender. But in moments of greatest anguish he himself would come to my help. As if conjured up by some magic world he stood amongst the slanderous monsters, towering above them all.

"Do you believe in me?" he asked, gazing at me with the apprehensive look and giving me his kindest smile.

"Yes, I believe," I answered, raising up these words as I had seen, when a child, the priest raise up the golden monstrance, and at that my host of tormentors grew quiet, as the congregation did at church.

Of all that my friend knew nothing.

Just as we had never in our personal intercourse said anything to disclose our innermost thought or feeling, our letters remained equally distant and cool, with perhaps only a line now and again, which failed to hide our longing or grief.

But on those lines we lived—or I at least. Those lines held out to me all and everything—imparted to my soul all the strength and sweetness that it needed to persuade the weary limbs to do their dull, daily work once more. And thus it happened that I was sometimes even happy, that, with a smile in my eyes, I cleaned the copper pots until they all shone, and scarcely felt the cold when, early on a winter morning, I knelt down to wash the steps outside the house. But the most beautiful moment was when in the evening I took my little savings-box and spread its contents on my bed. That money I regarded as my greatest treasure, always hiding it away most anxiously, and I should have been inconsolable if I had lost it by any mishap.

I was determined to leave Marlow as soon as I had saved all the money to cover my debt, and a little over to last me until I had found a suitable situation in London. Things, however, did not turn out in accordance with my expectations.

For some time back my mistress had intended to send her daughter to a school abroad, and all at once she made up her mind to do so. She did not care to live in the large house all by herself, and told me that she was going to shut it up and travel about. Since all the money I still wanted did not amount to more than fifty to sixty shillings, I felt much grieved when she told me of her intentions, because there was no possibility now of sending the money off in a few months as I had hoped to be able to do. But soon I grew more quiet about it, comforting myself with the hope of finding another situation very quickly, and of being able after all to return the money in the shortest time possible.

Thus it came to pass that I left the house, where for eighteen months I had been happy and unhappy in so peculiar a fashion; and when I looked round my room for the last time I felt the tears spring into my eyes, and I went downstairs sobbing bitterly. After having arrived in London, I went to the home to see my friend. She welcomed me most heartily, but could do nothing else for me. The next thing I wanted to do now was to find a situation in order to spend as little of my savings as possible.

I called again on the elderly lady who had given me my first post, and after the usual greetings and necessary explanations she said:

"Since you have been in England for some time, and also possess a reference given by an English lady, it will not be difficult to find something suitable for you. What kind of a situation do you prefer?"

I thought of the sixty shillings which I wanted to earn as quickly as possible, and said that I did not mind in the least, but should feel happy if I could get an opportunity to speak a little English.

"Should you like to take a post as an under-nurse?"

I had never heard of an under-nurse before, and did not quite know what she meant.

"What's an under-nurse?"

"Well, you would like it no doubt, because the head-nurse is an Englishwoman, so you would have plenty of opportunity to speak English."

After that I asked for the particulars, which she gave me in full.

"It is best for you," she said, "to go there and show yourself to the lady. If you like the post then well and good, but should you not care for it, then come back again."

She handed me the address and I went on my way. It seemed to be tremendously far, and when, after much looking and asking, I at last pulled the bell of a pretty house, I felt dead tired. A neat-looking parlour-maid inquired my wishes, invited me to step in, and told me to wait. I sat down on one of the upright oak chairs, and in my heart of hearts hoped that the lady might not come immediately. But she appeared very soon, and was most kind and gracious. After she had asked me a few questions she told me that she would like to engage me, but could not do so before the head-nurse had seen me. But the head-nurse was out with the children, so would I either wait or come again? I decided to wait, after which she left me to myself, and inwardly I prayed to God that He might make the head-nurse like me too. A little while afterwards I could hear much shouting and yelling, and the lady came in to tell me that the head-nurse had returned. She asked me to follow her upstairs, where we were met by four boys, aged about five, seven, nine, and eleven years, who had come to some disagreement which they seemed unable to put right. A very thin-looking woman, whom I guessed to be the head-nurse, tried to quiet them, a task that proved only successful after she had produced a long cane, the sight of which had an immediate effect upon the four brothers. The head-nurse put the cane very carefully into a corner and listened attentively to what her mistress told her about me. Now and again she looked at me, and with much comfort and relief I noticed that she seemed to like me.

The lady then explained to me what I would have to do, and I felt a growing alarm the longer she spoke. But when she asked me in the end whether I would like to take the post, I thought again of the sixty shillings and said I should like to come.

I started my new situation two days later. If I had no idea of the position of an under-nurse before, I was to get it now. I found out quickly that among the four servants of the house, I was considered to be the most insignificant one, and each of the three other servants made me feel this. Owing to the fact that I spoke English imperfectly, and neither the cook nor the parlour-maid were fond of foreigners, they teased and taunted me at every possible opportunity. Furthermore, they made me do all the work that they themselves did not care to do, such as bringing up coal from the cellar and so forth. In order to get on with them, I did everything. But the nights proved to be even more terrible than the days. I had to sleep in one room with the cook and the parlour-maid, and many times I set my teeth when I thought of my own little room at Marlow. The two girls used to chat together until midnight, relating all about their lovers, and mentioning, I am sure, every Christian name for boys which is to be found in the calendar. The one of whom I was the most afraid was the cook. She was terribly rude, and often raised her hands as if to beat me whenever I did not do a thing to her entire satisfaction.

However, every cup of sorrow contains its drop of mirth, and my happiness arose from the cook's outings and her love-letters. The fact is that when she received a letter from one of her many adorers she was kind even to me.

One day a soldier presented her with a silver brooch, and she was so nice that day to me that I almost liked her in the evening. But when it happened that a day or more passed without having brought her a token of some kind she became furious, and her spiteful rage was beyond all bounds. While I still lived at Marlow I had often stood and watched for the postman, hoping secretly that he might bring something for me, but now I stood and watched for him, filled only with the ardent longing that he might have something for the cook; and I think that now is the right moment, and here the right place, to express my thanks to all the policemen, soldiers, milkmen, butchers and others, who were happy enough to come within scope of the cook's interest and consideration, for the numbers of letters and cards which they despatched to her without knowing that they had made me happy too.

One day there was a great row in the kitchen, and the parlour-maid left the same day. The new parlour-maid was a very pale and ill-looking girl, but she worked very hard. She was never rude to me. I liked her for that and felt sorry for her because she looked so weak. One evening, when the cook had her outing, and we lay alone in our room, the parlour-maid began to sob most piteously.

"What's the matter?" I asked her, and after some hesitation she told me that her sweetheart was lying on the point of death in a hospital for consumption. Then she pulled a letter from behind her pillow and handed it over to me. I lit the candle and by its flickering light I read the lines. Brave yet desperate words of a dying man, together with a poem, which throbbed with the unspeakable longing for health and life, and disclosed the most sweet and most lovable thoughts.

"I am sure," I said, trying hard to conceal my emotion—"I am sure he will get well again."

"No; he is there where only the dying are."

Her eyes were dry when she said that, and only her lips trembled. I put out the light and shuddered. From that evening onward I helped her as much as I could with her work, although I had plenty to do myself.

One night she roused us from our sleep with a terrible scream, and looking round her wildly, she said she was sure that "he" had called for her. On the morning she asked for half a day off, but she returned no more.

After I had been at my post for about six months, I went one day to the post-office to have a letter registered. The letter was addressed to my friend in Buda-Pesth and contained the money which I owed to him. But it contained something else beside that—the outcry of a heart tortured to death. For the first time I told him of my unbearable position. He wrote back at once. His letter was full of kind reproaches for my silence about so many facts—what he termed my insincerity. He further urged me to leave my place at once, take no situation whatsoever, and give myself up entirely to the study of the English language in order to be able to go in for an examination afterwards. He also returned the money which I had sent, begging me to use it for board and so on. Further sums would follow.

It happened that it was my day out when I received the letter, and I went to see my friend in the home. I showed her the letter from Buda-Pesth, and she greatly urged me to accede to his wishes.

"I know what men are like," she said, "and I feel convinced that that man means to deal honestly with you."

In this way she spoke to me for a long while, and being afraid to take a new situation on account of the cooks, I at last consented. My friend then told me that she had thought of leaving the home, and suggested that we should take one room together.

"It would be cheapest," she argued.

I liked the idea because, as she said, "it was cheapest," and thus it happened that I packed up my things once more and moved into a boarding-house in London, my heart filled with joyous hopes.

It is true that it worried me again to owe money to my friend in Buda-Pesth. I consoled myself, however, with the intention to work very hard in order to pass an examination in the English language very soon, and then—Yes, and then! All at once I stopped to think. The old, well-known hobgoblins appeared once more, and sneered and grinned at me out of every corner. I pulled myself together with all the self-restraint possible, shook off every thought for the future and studied very hard.

The life in the boarding-house was full of interest and liveliness. The boarders belonged to different races and spoke different languages.

There were, for instance, Indians, wearing turbans of white or daintily shaded silk; Chinese, who had, however, sacrificed their pigtails to the fashion of Europe; a former prima donna who had grown too stout for the stage, and showed, with much fondness, photos of herself in stage costumes; a pale, worn-out-looking gentleman from Switzerland who could not put up with the fact that no English girl—unlike some French girls of his acquaintance—would undertake the management of his own household without the usual vows at the altar; a German who could not stand the English cooking; and a young striving musician who was unable to pay for his board and tried to commit suicide every Saturday.

Although the people were polite to me and I liked them very well, I did not really care to associate much with them. Such, however, was not the case with my friend, who used to amuse herself chiefly with the discontented Swiss, in a way that at first surprised, later alarmed, and finally disgusted me. It happened often that I left the dining-room without a word, and sat down on my bed in our little room until my friend came upstairs. She then used to look very gay and began to tell me stories such as I had never heard from her before, and which recalled to me the stories of the cook. I responded but little, whereupon she grew very bad-tempered, and declared I was a dull girl who could never see a joke. Sometimes I felt some sharp reply on the tip of my tongue, but swallowed it down again, thinking that I was perhaps really "dull" and she right after all. I tried to make amends for my behaviour by greater attention and tenderness towards her, showing also much interest for the stories she told me. In reality, however, I found everything most tedious, and would have much preferred to talk about poems. But my friend had declared once for all that she did not care for poems. Thus I tried hard to keep up our friendship, which was no more than a comedy, and should no doubt have kept it up even longer if she had not done something which put an end to my uncomfortable position.

I had gone upstairs rather early one evening and left my friend in the company of the other boarders. I was in bed when she came up at last. She looked frightfully hot and was shaking with laughter.

"What's the matter?" I asked her with affected interest.

Still laughing, she pulled out a crumpled sheet of newspaper and straightened it.

"No, I never!" she exclaimed. "You must read that."

I looked at the paper and saw that it was French.

"How can I read it? I don't know French."

"Oh well, I forgot; I will read it out to you."

"But I can't understand it."

"Never mind; I am going to translate it."

After that, she placed herself close to my bed and read out a story which made me furious.

"Stop, if you please," I said; "I will hear no more of it."

She laughed aloud.

"You are only acting now; the truth is that you are anxious to hear the end."

"No; I will hear no more," I said decidedly; and because she did not stop I got out of bed and ran, barefooted as I was, into the bathroom close by. I stayed there for rather a long while, and when I came back she was in bed and pretended to be asleep. I knew, however, that it was impossible for us to live together any longer. We did not speak to each other next morning. As soon as I had dressed, I went out and took a room for myself in quite a different part of London.

I lived now close to Westminster Abbey.

I had heard much about it already, but had not yet seen it, and determined to visit that place at the first possible moment.

With my heart beating fast, I stood a few days later in front of its grey, sacred walls, and a little later I slipped in and mixed with the swarm of visitors. I did not, however, walk about as they did, but pressed myself hard into the first corner. Never in all my life had I felt what I felt then. I was like one spellbound, as if I was in immediate personal touch with all those who had been there a long, long time ago, and who were nothing but dust now.

I roused myself at last and moved on. But I walked about like a sleep-walker, conceiving only the infinite greatness of all things, hardly realizing the reality of what I saw.

After some wandering to and fro I caught sight suddenly of a low, little wooden door, and thought of opening it. I looked round carefully because I did not know whether it was permitted (it is permitted), pushed it open quickly and went out. Yes, really and truly out! Then, lo and behold! behind that door there was no chapel filled with coffins or monuments of kings and queens, but a garden in the shape of a square, which, it is true, had no flowers, but a beautiful, well-kept lawn, and that piece of green garden looked wonderful amid those grey, massive walls, which, could they but speak, are able to tell the stories of many a century. A few benches were placed here and there and I sat down. I knew that the Abbey itself had once upon a time been a monastery, and guessed that this had been the convent garden. I imagined that I could see the tall figures of the monks leaving the dormitory, proceeding slowly over the sparkling lawn, and disappearing behind the little door to attend their early morning service.

Whenever I visited Westminster Abbey later on (I am glad to say I did that very often) I paid my homage first to the tombs, the old, old coronation chair, the famous stone beneath it, which is regarded as the stone on which Jacob had slept and dreamt his world-known dream, the Poets' Corner, and to countless other glorious things; after which I restrained no longer the sweet impatience of my heart, but slipped through the low wooden door into the convent garden. And seated there on one of the benches, with my eyes twinkling, because of the full, sudden glare of light, I used to weave some sweet sad tale of love around the sombre figure of a proud and handsome monk.

Apart from these hours of so sweet, restful, and contemplative a nature, every day was given up to work. I did all in my power to acquaint myself most thoroughly with a knowledge of the English language, and made such good progress that I began to compose my verses in English. It is true that these poems will most probably never secure me the gratitude of the

English people, but nevertheless they pleased me much, and my friend too expressed his satisfaction with them. He also sometimes asked me now what I was going to do after I had passed my examination, whether I was intending to stay in England or to go somewhere else.

But to these questions I never wrote any answer, and when I had to do so at last, a similar cowardice got hold of me to that which possessed St. Peter when he denied his Master.

"Do you think that I may come back?" I asked him.

Later on I went to post the lines, and when I returned to my room I found all the old well-known witches again.

"Is not something that is good beyond questioning—not clear as the purest water?"

Thus they whispered into my ear high and low in every scale, and beside that whisper I could hear the church bell strike every hour of the night.

The days seemed to creep to the thrilling impatience within me, and sometimes I felt a sudden terror at an unknown dread.

"What will he write to me? And when will he write?" I asked myself over and over again.

His letter arrived at last; it was put in a blue envelope and felt like a weight of lead in my hand. I could not make up my mind to open it, and wished somehow that I had not yet received it.

Tearing open the envelope at last, I read the letter, read it again and again. When I dropped the neatly written sheets, there was a dead stillness in the room. Involuntarily I looked around me. All the evil spirits had gone. All fear, all cowardice, all doubt had gone. Something like a cloud lifted from my soul, and then a feeling rose up to which I could as yet give no name, a feeling which tumbled about within me like someone aroused from a dream, and finally pressed itself hard against my throat.

I put my arms on the table, my face on my arms, and sat still for a long while. When it had grown dark and late I hid the letter underneath my pillow, and went to sleep without a light in the room. Once during the night I sat up in bed and lit a candle, and then I took the letter and holding it close to the light looked for one passage:

"If you had remained here, I do not know what might have happened; if you come back, I know what will happen. But the question is, may it come thus? You are not a girl of the ordinary type; you belong to the race of Asra, the people who die when they love. And because I have known that from the first, I have done for you what I have never done for another woman yet—namely, got hold of the head of the beast within, turned it round sharply and laughed at it."

I hid the letter again and lay very still in my bed.... That then was the end of it.... Tired and reluctantly my thoughts pilgrimaged back. I saw myself again as I was—poor, lonesome, waiting until the moment when the fairest miracle which life has ever held came to me, and every thought within me stretched forth arms, as it were, in order to receive it. I felt once more how every word, every look of his, pressed itself into my soul like a red-hot seal, and I suffered anew all the tortures and all the happiness. And all at once I thought again of the story of "Morgan" and of his young wife.... How truly different an ending, and yet how similar a victory! For which was more glorious for a girl—that a man should make her his wife, or make her his most beautiful dream, and his lasting desire? And all that I vainly tried to comprehend before I comprehended now. "Yes," I said to myself—and I said it aloud into the darkness of the room—"discontented, restless, aimless, freed from one passion to-day, and chained to another passion to-morrow, thus will he stagger through his life. Ever full of desire, never at peace with himself, he will taste of every pleasure and get to know every disgust. But above all pleasure and above all disgust there will be the one longing of his soul, which had denied itself the drink, because of the dregs it knew to be at the goblet's bottom. Not while in ecstasy, not in the hustle and bustle of the day will he be aware of it—nay, but when he lies awake at night, filled with a sense of utter loneliness, listening to the pouring rain outside, then it will come to life again, will throb and tremble through his soul, soft and pleading like an old forgotten strain." And after I had said that, I smiled that strange wonderful smile, which only a woman knows who is willing to take upon herself the heaviest burden for the sweet sake of love.

Next morning I left the house very early and wandered through the streets of London. To-day I knew that I would wander through those streets many, many times yet, and for a long, long while.

Once I stopped and entered a grey, small building. It was a Roman Catholic church. I walked about it aimlessly, and my eyes caught the picture of Christ in life-size. For the first time in my life, perhaps, the sight of it stirred nothing within me. What use could He be to me? Could He comprehend such a thing at all? It is true that He had become human in order to feel with us, but He was a good man. He only knew the sins and passions of others, never did He know a sin, or a passion of His own. Of godly descent. He was endowed with godly strength, with godly wisdom, with godliness. What did He really know of the nature of a thief, of a murderer, of a perjurer? And though He had died for the sake of love, what did He know of the sufferings of lovers?

I turned away from the picture and went out of the church. I went out on tip-toe by force of habit, but on my soul dawned the religion of life, which is older than the doctrine of Jesus ... and all round me walked its disciples. Men and women who had done with dreaming and were ready for the unknown hereafter—men with strong fists and hard looks, by which one could tell that they had battled with life; women whose faces looked wrinkled and worn, telling their story of hardship and silent surrender; men and women who in their days of severity and bitterness had surpassed the miracles wrought by Him, the Galilean; men and women among whose numbers I was also enlisted.

And out of that new consciousness arose to me a new wisdom and a new love—a wisdom which reigned over all former wisdom, and a love which reigned over all former love. And when I returned with it into my solitude, the stones began to speak.